### *"This isn't a dream?"*

Rachel asked softly.

"No." Just to prove it, Luke leaned over her, intending merely to brush his lips against hers. A moment later he was trailing kisses down the side of her face, a fierce hunger igniting inside him.

Her eyes were still closed so he couldn't tell what she was thinking. He stroked her head, marvelling at the silky softness of her hair. Her scent infiltrated his nostrils, reminding him of summer roses.

"Rachel," he said at last, his voice husky with emotion. "I don't want you to leave."

"I—I don't know what to say."

"Try...I want to stay, Luke," he suggested.

D0250067

Dear Reader,

When I think of the month of June, I summon up images of warm spring days with the promise of summer, joyous weddings and, of course, the romance that gets the man of your dreams to the point where he can celebrate Father's Day.

And that's what June 1990 is all about here at Silhouette Romance. Our DIAMOND JUBILEE is in full swing, and this month features *Cimarron Knight*, by Pepper Adams—the first book in Pepper's *Cimarron Stories* trilogy. Hero Brody Sawyer gets the shock of his life when he meets up with delightful Noelle Chandler. Then in July, don't miss *Borrowed Baby*, by Marie Ferrarella. Brooding loner Griffin Foster is in for a surprise when he finds that his sister has left him with a little bundle of joy!

The DIAMOND JUBILEE—Silhouette Romance's tenth anniversary celebration—is our way of saying thanks to you, our readers. To symbolize the timelessness of love, as well as the modern gift of the tenth anniversary, we're presenting readers with a DIAMOND JUBILEE Silhouette Romance title each month, penned by one of your favorite Silhouette Romance authors. In the coming months, many of your favorite writers, including Lucy Gordon, Dixie Browning, Phyllis Halldorson and Annette Broadrick, are writing DIAMOND JUBILEE titles especially for you.

And that's not all! There are six books a month from Silhouette Romance—stories by wonderful authors who time and time again bring home the magic of love. During our jubilee year, each book is special and written with romance in mind. June brings you *Fearless Father*, by Terry Essig, as well as *A Season for Homecoming*, the first book in Laurie Paige's duo, *Homeward Bound*. And much-loved Diana Palmer has some special treats in store in the months ahead.

I hope you'll enjoy this book and all the stories to come. Come home to romance—Silhouette Romance—for always!

Sincerely,

Tara Hughes Gavin
Senior Editor

# GEETA KINGSLEY

# Faith, Hope and Love

Published by Silhouette Books New York

**America's Publisher of Contemporary Romance**

For Bob
protector of the flame

SILHOUETTE BOOKS
300 E. 42nd St., New York, N.Y. 10017

Copyright © 1990 by Geeta M. Kakade

All rights reserved. Except for use in any review, the reproduction or utilization of this work in whole or in part in any form by any electronic, mechanical or other means, now known or hereafter invented, including xerography, photocopying and recording, or in any information storage or retrieval system, is forbidden without the permission of Silhouette Books, 300 E. 42nd St., New York, N.Y. 10017

ISBN: 0-373-08726-8

First Silhouette Books printing June 1990

All the characters in this book are fictitious. Any resemblance to actual persons, living or dead, is purely coincidental.

®: Trademark used under license and registered in the United States Patent and Trademark Office and in other countries.

Printed in the U.S.A.

## GEETA KINGSLEY

feels one doesn't have to be perfect at things to enjoy doing them. Singing (off key), art (dot-to-dot pictures), homemaking (it takes real willpower to ignore dirty dishes and dust), and gardening (watching things grow) are all on her love-to-do list.

Her gypsy karma has led to travels all over the world. Home at present is California, where she lives with her husband and teenage son and daughter. Reading and writing stories have always been an important part of her life. A former elementary school teacher, her job title these days is professional dreamer.

OREGON

NEVADA

● San Francisco

● Monterey

**CALIFORNIA**

● The Diamond Bar
● Santa Barbara
● Ventura
● Los Angeles
Santa Barbara Islands

*Pacific Ocean*

● San Diego

MEXICO

Underlined places are fictitious.

# Chapter One

The moment Luke saw her he knew he'd won.

There was no way the judge would award custody of Gordie to this woman. Rachel Carstairs looked as if a breeze would blow her away...he'd seen will-o'-the-wisps with more substance.

His gaze raced up patent leather shoes, slim ankles, nice legs, the anonymous drape of a raw silk suit and screeched to a halt.

The face. She looked as if she'd just been through the wring cycle of a washing machine. Twice. Her pronounced pallor drew him to her eyes. Gray verging on black, their expression transfixed him. They appeared to be lanced with strain. Lanced with something else he couldn't define. If he had to guess, he would put it down as acute apprehension. The blond hair pulled back off her face in some sort of knot accentuated her fragility. Her slimness underscored it.

Rachel Carstairs had aimed for poise and sophistication. She'd achieved the look of a child playing dress up. She looked as if she needed taking care of herself...as if she wanted this to be over as much as he did.

What he saw, added to what he knew about her, equaled defeat. Hers.

The head-on encounter lasted for one beat of a hummingbird's wings. In that second Luke absorbed signs of stress that grated on his already tense nerves. She was as taut as copper wire in a fuse box.

The sight of her belied his original thought that she was after money. Luke had inherited his grandfather's shrewdness in assessing people. The ability had never served him wrong. This child-woman was an innocent.

The thought that maybe in some curious way she wanted Gordie just for the baby's sake, was like sand in his eyes. Seeing her, put a face on an image he'd found easy to hate. When he'd been informed she was taking him to court over custody of his nephew he had been furious. Now the image her action had sketched, of a selfish, conniving woman, had to be deleted. Rachel Carstairs looked as defenseless as his ten-month-old-nephew.

Her lawyer steered her a little to one side, talking earnestly. Luke's eyes flickered incredulously over her choice of legal representation and he let out a long heavy breath. The man looked as if this was his first case...as if he needed a hand to hold himself.

Babes in the wood, the pair of them. Instinct wove uneasiness into Luke's premise. This whole thing was turning into a farce.

Rachel looked at the man's broad back as he went into the courtroom. *That* was Luke Summers? He seemed capable of bringing up a dozen children on his own...and enjoying it. The epitome of sturdy dependability, he showed her up like light did flaws.

For one impossible moment when their glances had collided, she'd felt he was offering her more than met the eye. Sympathy, understanding, *friendship*. Rachel shook her head to clear it. They were antagonists. Jet lag was affecting her hormones strangely. Strength and power reaching out to cocoon her had to be a figment of her overtired imagination.

Fear threaded through her brain and she wondered if her urge to return, to fight for custody of Chris's son had all been one big mistake.

She'd imagined a man holding onto the child out of duty, resenting him as he grew, as her own father had resented her after her mother had left. She hadn't wanted that to happen to Gordie. Now intuition yelled that she'd presumed too much. She had a suspicion intuition was right.

Fatigue tugged at her like an insidious tide. Rachel fought the urge to give way to it. If she as much as closed her eyes now she would prove that human beings could fall asleep on their feet.

The plane from Bangladesh had been delayed in Hong Kong for twenty-four hours. Purported as engine trouble, rumor heightened tension by hinting at the threat of a bomb. By the time they'd finally landed at Los Angeles International Airport it had been six-thirty this morning. The hearing was scheduled for eleven in Santa Barbara. She'd called Dyan Jenks, her lawyer, from MRA headquarters in Bangladesh just before leaving the country. When she'd asked why the hearing couldn't be held in Los Angeles, he'd mumbled something about jurisdiction and the law. The Diamond Bar, where Gordie lived now, was in Santa Barbara County, and so the hearing would be held in the Santa Barbara County Superior Courthouse.

Which meant her journey wasn't finished at LAX. Hurrying through Customs, Rachel had inquired about flights to Santa Barbara and rushed to a national terminal.

Her luggage hadn't presented a problem. She had none. Just a backpack, stuffed with toilet articles and a rumpled change of clothing.

It had taken forty-six tense minutes, airborne, to get to Santa Barbara Municipal Airport. Hurling herself into a taxi, she'd explained the reason for haste to the driver. Tuning into her urgency with the enthusiasm of a man starved for adventure, he'd made it in record time to the nearest mall and agreed to wait for her.

In the closest store Rachel had grabbed the first suit she'd seen in her size, some shoes and a pair of stockings. Paying for them had eaten into her precious hoard of traveler's checks. Changing out of her travel-stained pants and top had eaten into her precious time. But it had to be done. She had to project respectability.

Jumping into the waiting cab, Rachel had tried to breathe deeply, relax. The snarled traffic didn't help. Her heartbeats measured each passing second aloud as her last conversation with her counsel came to mind. Calling him from Hong Kong had been an experience in itself. The conversation had been punctuated with static but the message had been clear. If she didn't make it, they would lose.

The cab had spilled her out at the steps of the courthouse at exactly ten-forty-five and her lawyer had introduced himself. Vaguely she'd noted the exterior of the courthouse looked like a castle out of a picture book.

She looked at Dyan now and felt her fear increase. He was nothing like the assured woman with Luke Summers. He looked as nervous as she felt, his restless pacing and uneasy smiles not helping her waning self-confidence the slightest bit.

Myrna Hasting's hand on Luke's sleeve indicated it was time to go in. He wished the woman would stick to words to communicate with. He was in no mind for body language, with it's accompanying insinuation that his lawyer had a large hole in her private life that he would fill nicely.

Entering the courtroom Luke looked around. The judge had agreed to a closed courtroom, which meant at least they wouldn't have a crowd gaping at them, as well as unwanted publicity.

The room wasn't very large. One glance encompassed the rows of seats, the wooden railing separating the principal players from the rest of the room. Two large tables, four feet apart, faced the massive oak desk behind which the judge would preside. The flags of the United States and the state of California flanked the wall behind the judge's chair. The room reeked of judicial solemnity, the portent atmosphere making Luke even more restless.

What he really needed was air. Of the kind untainted with drama. He was just an ordinary man with an ordinary ideal. Live and let live. He'd coped with his brother and sister-in-law's death, with the dramatic change in his life-style. He'd taken to instant fatherhood, although nothing in his bachelor life had prepared him for it. To accept what couldn't be changed took maturity not sentiment. He had plenty of the former and doing what had to be done came naturally. But this heaped helping of drama he could have done without.

The woman's assumption that she could walk in and take Gordie as if he were a box of chocolates had enraged him. As far as Luke knew, Gordie's mother—his sister-in-law Chris—had seen this cousin only once when they were both children. Rachel Carstairs's only communication had been brief scrawls on exotic postcards. She hadn't come to the wedding or visited Chris once at the ranch.

What was the group she worked for called? MRA? It was some sort of relief organization. The thought that she wanted money for her good deeds had been the only other reason for her claiming custody of Gordie he'd been able to come up with. Imagination had sketched a picture of a missionary type with a pith hat, khaki trousers, leathery skin and a burning zeal to change the world.

Rachel Carstairs looked as if she couldn't change her shoes without help.

Luke let out another heavy sigh. There was no sense in getting riled up now. He needed to keep a clear head on his shoulders, say the right things. Turmoil wasn't like him. Neither was worrying over a perfect stranger.

The courtroom closed in on him. The collar of his one-hundred-percent cotton shirt irked him. The gray wool suit irked him. The whole damn world irked him. The designer tie felt like a choke chain. He wrangled with the urge to yank it off. Myrna had insisted appearances counted. He stood and went outside.

Why should the future of a baby hang on a stranger's decision? What did a dealer in black-and-white justice know about emotions as delicate as spun silk? About a baby that looked at you with your dead brother's eyes? About commitment and honor? About last wishes that no one had thought necessary to legalize? About love.

Judge Erica Wentworth, Myrna had assured him, was the best. She wouldn't be swayed by the fact that he was a man, and a single one at that. It was no longer taken for granted that women were automatically better parents. Rachel Carstairs would have to prove a great many other things first. He had so much more weighing in his favor. Commitment, dependability, affluence.

One could never be sure, though. Luke couldn't afford to take any chances where Gordie was concerned. Misgivings nagged like a strand of chicken caught in his teeth—in an unreachable spot.

Women tended to side with women. What if the judge didn't think a man capable of nurturing an infant. What if Rachel Carstairs used her haunted eyes as weapons. What if the real issue was lost in appearances and assumptions.

The real issue was love. He loved Gordie. The ten-month-old baby was all he had left of his brother. Luke's grief had emerged from the chrysalis of shock, as fully fledged determination. He wanted Gordie to grow up on the ranch, in the shade of his care. He wanted the child to know his heritage. He wanted nothing bad to ever touch Gordie's life again.

Myrna's smile of welcome as he returned to his seat put him in mind of a fat cat that gets to choose between a canary and cream. Any minute now she would start purring and washing her face.

"Did you get a look at her?"

He'd gotten two. The second one had shown her sitting apart from her counsel. Not talking. Not moving. Her counsel was saying something. Luke felt she wasn't listening.

"We've won."

For the first time since he'd hired Myrna, Luke was irritated by her self-possession. The woman was a barracuda.

He wanted Gordie. Not blood.

The judge's entrance fast forwarded the drama. Luke detached himself from the scene, willing himself into the role of impartial outsider. It was the best way he knew to help himself.

Both counsels presented their cases. Both clients wanted the same thing. Custody of ten-month-old Gordon Summers.

He was called to the stand, reminded of the oath he'd taken. Myrna gave him an "it's-in-the-bag" smile and Luke realized he hated rapacious women with too white teeth. But then he'd wanted the best lawyer.

"Mr. Summers would you share with the court, the details of the twentieth of July?"

Luke cleared his throat. His eyes swerved to Rachel Carstairs. She sat on the edge of her seat. For the first time she was looking straight at him. Not through him. Her bitumen eyes were twin drills, boring into his brain.

"I was spending the weekend on the ranch I co-owned with my late brother." The words conjured instant pain. "My brother and sister-in-law had decided to fly to Palm Springs for a charity gala." Another pause, longer this time. The muscle throbbing in his jaw made it difficult to sound matter-of-fact. "Their plane crashed ten minutes after takeoff. It exploded on impact. There were no survivors."

He looked her way again. Her stillness tugged at him. Both arms were wrapped around her body. As if she were cold. As if she wanted to shut out the scene he'd just painted. In that moment Luke knew that she'd loved Chris. The thought landed on the top of his already high pile of doubts, escalating his uneasiness. They should have found another way of sorting out their differences.

"Thank you, Mr. Summers. Did your brother ever mention writing a new will after the birth of his son?"

"No." Rob's joy had made him oblivious to the fact that death didn't respect happiness.

"So, Gordon Summers has no legal guardian?"

"No."

"According to the will your brother made after he got married, he left everything to his wife. In the unlikely eventuality of their dying together, he named you as sole beneficiary. Is that right?"

"Yes."

"Will you tell the court about the latest provisions you have made for your nephew, Gordon Summers?"

Luke cleared his throat. They'd gone over this so many times but still the dammed words stuck in his throat.

"I've drawn up a deed gifting Gordon half of my ranch, the Diamond Bar. I have also formed a trust for him, with all the money my brother left. In the event of my death, while I'm single Gordon will be my legal heir, as well."

Luke hated the way it came out. He wasn't trying out for sainthood. He was just doing what had to be done.

Myrna wasn't through yet. "Mr. Summers what did you do after the tragedy?"

"I took a month's leave of absence from my job."

"To do what, Mr. Summers?"

"To be with the baby."

Did the judge have children? Did she know how much a baby could miss warm, loving parents? Gordie had fretted, lost weight, cried for no reason at all. His baby eyes had turned to the door everytime someone had come in. Searching for his parents, for the cherishing, comforting warmth of their presence.

"Why did you feel the need to take care of the baby yourself?" Myrna's eyes told him he was doing beautifully. Strange, he'd never noticed how cold eyes that particular shade of blue could be. "Surely someone else, a house-keeper, would have done just as well?"

"I have a housekeeper to help me. Hannah Rodriguez helped bring Rob and me up. I just wanted to be with Gordie."

"And now the one month is over, do you plan on going back to work?"

Myrna was sharp enough to cut herself.

"No. I plan on working from the ranch. Luckily, in my line of work it can be done."

"Isn't it true that this will affect your chances of promotion? That you were next in line for a vice presidency?"

"Yes."

She was really going all out.

"Isn't it also true that your boss agreed to your proposal if you took a pay cut?"

Damn. She was trying to make him appear a hero. There was no need for that. "Yes."

"So, why are you doing all this?" Self-confidence dripped from every word.

"Because I want more time with Gordie."

Myrna's smile was a masterpiece of triumph. "That will be all, Your Honor."

The opposing counsel approached him. He was asked if he was married, if he planned on marriage in the near future. None of the questions had one quarter the impact of Myrna's. Luke realized the man was even more ineffective than he'd first suspected.

Rachel Carstairs was called to the bench.

Luke frowned. He could have sworn she swayed. The little fool. Was she drunk? On drugs? She straightened so quickly, he didn't think anyone else had noticed.

Dyan Jenks was questioning her. "Ms. Carstairs would you tell the court where you were when you received the news of your cousin and her husband's death?"

"Bangladesh." She cleared her throat.

"When did you get the news?"

"The thirtieth of September."

"Why did it take almost nine weeks for the news of your cousin's death to reach you?"

"Letters always take a while to get to us. This one took longer than usual because we were in an area cut off by floods."

"What was your first reaction?"

"That I had to get back, take care of the baby."

"But you couldn't leave right away?"

"No. We were in an acute relief area. It took another five to six weeks after I received the news for the situation to be brought under some sort of control and extra help to arrive. I left as soon as I could."

Jenks nodded as if he'd just scaled Everest. "The defense rests, Your Honor."

The naive idiot. He hadn't even scratched the surface. Luke tightened his hand into a fist as Myrna got to her feet. A bloodhound closing in on its quarry couldn't have been more eager.

"Ms. Carstairs, were you and your cousin very close?"

A pause. "No."

"When was the last time you saw her?"

"When I was twelve."

"So, you were not at her wedding?"

"No."

"Ms. Carstairs will you tell the court what work you do?"

"I'm a medical aide with MRA, an organization that provides medical relief in disaster areas all over the world."

"And when did you join MRA?"

"Four and a half years ago."

"Since then you haven't returned to the States, even on vacation. Isn't that right?

"Yes."

"You have to look for a job here, don't you?"

"Yes."

"Tell me, Ms. Carstairs, do you own any property in the United States? An apartment, a condo, anything you can call home?"

"No."

"Ms. Carstairs have you ever taken care of a baby, other than in the course of your work?"

"No."

Luke shifted uneasily in his seat. Each reply was a nail in her coffin. Myrna's tones dripped honey as she moved in for the kill.

"Then how do you plan on taking care of your cousin's son?"

"I can learn." The statement held the punch of a feather.

"What are your job prospects, Ms. Carstairs? What will you and the baby live on while you get some kind of basic training? Who will you leave the baby with while you go to school? To work?"

"I have some money of my own."

"So, your plan is to take the baby from where he is well cared for, from people who love him, and leave him with a stranger or in a day-care center while you work. Do you think you can earn enough to rent a place and support yourself and a child, or do you plan on claiming welfare?"

"I can manage on what I have."

"Have you resigned from MRA, Ms. Carstairs?"

"No, I haven't thought as far—"

"Exactly," Myrna cut in triumphantly, "you haven't thought enough about anything. No further questions, Your Honor."

Luke expected anger, defeat, frustration. Some shred of emotion. He wasn't prepared for stoicism. There was no expression whatsoever on Rachel Carstairs's face as she stepped down. Who or what, Luke wondered thunderstruck, had taught her that kind of self-control?

Both lawyers presented closing statements. The judge declared a fifteen minute recess before rendering her decision.

He heard Jenks ask her if she would like to step outside, get a cup of coffee.

"No thank you."

Her voice bothered him. It didn't go with the rest of her. It was rusty, chipped, oddly husky. In such a short time it had gotten into his blood, a teasing torment—like a saloon girl in a fifties' western.

Her stance bothered him. She could have been carved into Mt. Rushmore. Not once had she looked around the courtroom, shown any interest in her surroundings. He'd been curious about her. Damn it, why wasn't she the same way?

The judge's decision was explicit. "Ms. Carstairs, I'm afraid wanting a child does not assure good parenting these days. Your life-style is not suited to an infant. The court feels of the two of you, Mr. Summers will be the better guardian. He will, I'm sure, be more than generous as far as visiting rights are concerned." Something in Rachel Carstairs's expression pierced the judge's formality. Her glance softened. "I'm sure on reflection you will agree with me that what Gordie needs is a settled home. Look at it this way. Instead of one, Gordie now has two caring adults interested in his welfare. If you could both combine forces with his interests at heart, everyone will be a winner."

Myrna's stranglehold, the smacking buss on his mouth, caught Luke off balance. By the time he got away from her, the bench beside theirs was empty.

He rushed out of the courtroom. The silent corridor yielded no clue to her whereabouts. On the steps of the courthouse he found Dyan Jenks staring at the taillights of a disappearing cab. Luke caught at the man's sleeve.

"Yes?"

"Ms. Carstairs. I need her address."

Dyan Jenks was not a good loser. "That's confidential information," he said pompously.

"I have some effects of her cousin's that she might like. Family mementos and so on. Give it to me." Luke was through explanations and into demanding.

Dyan hesitated. Luke Summers clearly didn't seem the kind to take no for an answer. Impatience snapped in the navy blue eyes. Irritation crackled from every pore. His clenched fist didn't look as if it could stay in his pocket much longer.

No one was paying him to be a hero.

"Are you familiar with State Street?"


Rachel knew it shouldn't hurt so much to lose something that had never been hers. Looking back now she'd done it all wrong.

Wrong clothes, wrong lawyer, wrong attitude. She was so full of hindsight she could write a how-not-to book.

A wry smile skimmed her lips as she thought of the hurdles she'd cleared in the past forty-eight hours, as well as the final result. She'd made it on time against innumerable odds. And lost.

Losing was a comfort zone, something she'd become used to. All her life.

Leaning against the black vinyl seat, Rachel let the events of the past few weeks race by her.

The first thing she'd done after hearing of the tragedy was send a telegram to the ranch, telling her cousin's brother-in-law she was arriving to care for the baby. Chris's mother had died two years ago. Her father was in a home for the terminally ill. As far as Rachel knew, she was Chris's only living relative capable of caring for the baby.

Luke Summers hadn't shared the opinion. His answering telegram had been equally long and explicit.

NO NEED TO RETURN STOP GORDIE IS MY RESPONSIBILITY NOW STOP BEST HE GROWS UP AT THE DIAMOND BAR STOP I INTEND TO START ADOPTION PROCEEDINGS IMMEDIATELY STOP VERY NICE OF YOU TO OFFER STOP

*Nice* hadn't been why she wanted Gordie. News of the tragedy had plunged her into the darkest despair. The one person who'd ever cared for her had been snatched away. In the blackness of her grief a pinprick of light had appeared, illuminating the path she had to take. By caring for Chris's son she could repay the one bright spot in her life: her cousin's love and friendship. Gordie would receive all the love stored in her heart for so long and finally she would have someone of her very own.

The brief smile that touched her lips mocked the pain she felt. Judge Wentworth's verdict was a rerun of her life story. Fate had again placed her outside the portal of a loving one-on-one relationship. The firm reminder that she didn't meet the criteria for membership in that particular club had been issued so often it shouldn't hurt at all. But it did.

She had to admire the skill with which Luke Summers's lawyer had made her look like a stupid, selfish woman. She wasn't entirely ignorant about a baby's needs. Nursing needy children had taught her a great deal about them. Often a really sick infant had been left with them for a couple of days, and it had been Rachel who had willingly played substitute mother.

Nor was she as destitute as they'd made her out to be. Her father had left her a lump sum of money. It would have provided for a place of her own and live-in help. Gordie wouldn't have lacked for anything. She would have seen he got the best.

Acting with the purest of instincts didn't buy one insurance against failure, though. The scene in the courtroom had left her with a bad taste in her mouth, a feeling of absolute inadequacy. The sooner she got back to the only work she was good at, the better.

Rachel bit her lip. By losing the case she felt she'd let Chris down and lost the opportunity to have someone to love. Someone of her very own. What was it Chris had said to her in one of her letters after the birth of her son? "I want you to be Gordie's godmother. You're the only one who will fit the role. We'll make it official when you come home."

Now, she wouldn't even have that.

The stereo in the cab blared out some discordant sounds. The latest music? She supposed so. The cabbie whistled while he checked the road for any tiny gap to leap into. Not that they made much progress, but evidently the man thought weaving was more fun than standing still. As Rachel looked out at the streets of Santa Barbara the scenes blurred. Her mind insisted on retracing the events that had culminated in today's defeat.

When she'd shown the telegram to Dr. Tom Atwell, the lead member of the team, he'd told her she needed a good lawyer. Dyan Jenks was the result of a long-distance telephone call to a friend of his. She'd hired him to start legal proceedings for custody of Christina's son. Hiring a lawyer long-distance hadn't been the best thing to do, but it had been the only option available. Dyan had been chosen by Tom Atwell's friend because he was Dr. Atwell's friend's nephew. No one had mentioned he was still wet behind the ears.

But blaming him was no use. She'd lost on her own account.

Like a rat on a treadmill, her mind refused to leave dejection alone. This whole incident was just another reminder that she was one of those destined to prove a human being *could* be an island. Rachel wondered detatchedly how long it would take her to learn her lesson and stop these futile attempts to have someone to belong to.

Her whole life was strewed with reminders, if she still needed them. Her mother hadn't wanted her. She'd left when Rachel was ten. Her father had had no use for her. At first she'd tried to make him like her. Later she'd known that was impossible and accepted it. There was no doubting it. She'd always gotten a failing grade in personal relations.

Best stick to what she could do well. Impersonal aid was her forte. Rachel let her mind trace over the past few years. In her last year in high school a volunteer with MRA had come to Wilson High. The slides he'd shown had been mind-boggling, the talk that followed powerful. There was a desperate need for medical aid abroad.

Rachel had been hooked by the lecture. Medical Relief Abroad had been started in the early seventies, by a group of doctors in America who had dedicated themselves to suffering humanity. From the original nucleus of ten the organization had grown to five thousand. It consisted entirely of volunteers.

While they were working, volunteers were provided with living expenses. When they returned after their tenure they were given a thousand dollars for each year spent abroad, and every assistance in job placement. Colleges offered special scholarships and grants to volunteers who wished to continue their education.

There had been no hint of glamour about the work. Dr. Steve Hanks had emphasized the rigors of living in undeveloped villages, the health hazards, the backbreaking work.

It called, he'd said, for a special kind of personal commitment.

Rachel had contacted him the following week. At the first interview it had been suggested she was too young, but Rachel had stood her ground. Convincing the selection committee that her slight build and frail looks were misleading had taken a while. The medical assistant's course she'd completed through the after school vocational program had helped. So had her counselor, Mrs. O'Brien, who'd convinced Dr. Hanks Rachel was mature enough for relief work.

A thorough medical examination had been followed by an intensive course in basic medical procedures. Her father hadn't objected to her going. If anything, he'd seemed relieved. The day after she'd graduated from high school, Rachel was on her way to Bangladesh—the stiff, awkward, unemotional parting with her father a frozen island of memory.

Work filled the void in her life, assuaging the physical loneliness. The gratitude shining out of dark eyes too poor to offer any other payment convinced her she'd found her niche. Immersing herself in the people, the work and the new way of life, Rachel told herself it was all she'd ever wanted. Very rarely did the thought that there was more to life than caring for others surface.

Over the years she and Dr. Atwell had been the only constant members of the team. A twelve-month stint was the norm for volunteers. Whenever the others had talked of home and plans for the future, Rachel had kept very quiet. Every year she'd applied for, and been granted an extension. Her accumulated vacation time she'd spent traveling in neighboring Nepal, and the north of India on cheap railway tickets, and in buses.

The telegram informing her of Chris and Rob's death had taken weeks to reach her. The team had been up to their eyeballs in disaster relief. The floods had wreaked havoc in a country that had barely learned to toddle. There was so much to do. But for Rachel it had been time to come home.

Tom had contacted two doctors with private practices in Los Angeles, both of whom had agreed to help her. Now it was no longer necessary to get in touch with them. The money she had left would last till she got on the next plane back to Bangladesh. Back to the only life she knew.

She was drunk from exhaustion. Lack of sleep, lack of food, lack of spirit. That's what made losing Gordie seem like the end. After she got some sleep she would be fine. The judge had been right. She was definitely not the best thing for the baby.

The uncle was certainly that. She tried to remember what he'd looked like. Solid. Large. *Rich*. And very, very sure of himself. The whiplash of his gaze had cut through her charade of respectability. A shiver crept down her spine. In that instant she'd felt wrapped in strength and power. The urge to reach out for some of each had been very strong.

What was even more bizarre was the powerful surge of response deep inside her wanting to believe her first impression was true. That if she *had* leaned into his strength she would have found the shelter she'd been searching for all her life.

## Chapter Two

Ma'am?"

Rachel sat up with a jerk. The cabbie was looking at her curiously. They were outside the motel. Dyan had reserved her a room here earlier. As she took in the peeling paint, the cracked sign, Rachel knew it fit all her prerequisites. Cheap, cheap and cheap. Her lawyer had scored a bull's-eye on this task at least. Tomorrow she would go to MRA headquarters in Los Angeles and transfer into their hostel. For tonight this would do.

Reluctance accompanied her as she stepped out of the cab's dark, comforting interior. She still had to go through the ordeal of checking in. The world tilted to a forty-five degree angle. Rachel stumbled and clung to the door. She ought to have grabbed a bite to eat somewhere.

"Are you all right?" the cabbie asked worriedly.

"I'm fine."

Rachel paid him, added a generous tip. He looked amazed, then overwhelmed. She was glad. Money had never meant much to her. Where she was going, she wouldn't need it anyway.

"Merry Christmas, ma'am."

Christmas. That was right. Four weeks to Christmas.

"And to you."

Empty, meaningless words. Empty meaningless life.

The clerk at the desk found her key right away. Yes, her room was in a quiet area. Yes, they would hold all calls.

Rachel walked to her room in a daze. The corridor seemed never ending, the smells nauseating. The key turned smoothly. It was the first thing that had gone right today, she thought hysterically. Someone ought to make a note of it. Tears trembled on her lower lids, waiting for an excuse to fall. She wouldn't let them. She was past crying.

A shower would be nice. It had been so long since her last one.

Incongruous thoughts pierced her fatigue like mismatched pieces of different puzzles. She had no other clothes with her. The travel weary pant and shirt she'd worn since Hong Kong were left behind in the changing rooms of some department store. The wallpaper in here was ugly. She hated that shade of mud brown, bilious green and jaundiced yellow. Chris's baby would be fine. That man looked like "auld lang syne" and the national anthem rolled into one. Imagine using those colors for cabbage roses...if she weren't so tired she would have insomnia just looking at them. All she had now was the handbag she'd transferred her traveler's checks and passport to and an empty rucksack. Nothing else. It was a good thing she had a return ticket.

The need for sleep edged out the need to feel clean. Rachel's footsteps changed direction. She could sleep for a week.

The knock on the door seemed a joke. Cruel, worthless and unnecessary. She wouldn't answer.

"Ms. Carstairs. Open up. I have to talk to you."

It was her name that did it. Only Dyan Jenks knew where she was. He wouldn't contact her if it wasn't important.

"Yes?" Her head was a wedge in the door. Even Emily Post wouldn't insist on courtesy after thirty-six hours without sleep. No one was going to get in here without a good reason. Not even the President of the United States.

"I'm Luke Summers. I have to talk to you."

The door swung open as if by magic.

He walked past her, turned and waited. Swaying on her feet, Rachel put a hand behind her for the couch and sank weightlessly into it. No, sitting would have her asleep quicker than one could say Jack and Jill. She struggled to her feet.

She had to think straight. She wasn't new to fatigue. They'd never adhered to working hours in the places she had been in. Lines of people formed magically at first light. Patient, suffering, hopeful. The team worked till the light faded or the last patient was attended to. Whichever came first. Rachel tapped into that same reserve of sheer willpower now. This might be her last chance to win Gordie. Maybe this man would listen. Maybe she ought to tell him what the child represented.

Rachel looked at him. Strange. He had no face at all. Just shimmering waves. Someone had stolen his face. She had to let him know so he could do something about it. Only her tongue was stuck to the roof of her mouth. She looked again. Now his face was just one big blank of silver. Like the floods in Bangladesh. Angry water reflecting cruel sunshine. Hypnotizing. Will sapping. *Dominating*.

Her eyelids fell. Rachel crumpled.

"Damn!"

He'd caught her just in time. What was wrong? Had his earlier suspicion been correct? Leaning forward, Luke smelled her breath. There was absolutely no trace of liquor.

She weighed less than a day-old foal. Luke strode into the bedroom and placed her on the covers. The little fool. She should have told someone how she felt. What if he hadn't decided to come and talk to her right away? She could have lain here forever.

Half an hour later Luke had the emergency ward of the nearest hospital on their toes. If he'd said jump, they would all have executed perfect leaps. He'd threatened them with everything from libel to unwanted publicity. He wanted attention and he wanted it now. No, he wouldn't leave the patient and wait outside. For once in their lives they could damn well live up to their category.

A lion with a sore tooth would have been more amenable.

A Dr. Andrews, finally armed with the results of some tests, approached him warily. Rachel Carstairs was suffering from only one thing. Exhaustion.

It made all the other little pieces fall into place. The whitewashed look, the stumbling.

"She isn't unconscious, just asleep. Probably the best medicine. Seems to have been running on nervous energy for too long. Hasn't eaten for the last twenty four hours, as well. We could start an intravenous drip and keep her overnight."

The doctor checked the large man's face for a reaction, wondering about his relationship to the patient. Ms. Carstairs was one lucky woman. Luke Summers had watched the tests they'd run on her like a mother hawk. One wrong move, his expression had warned, and I'll pull this place down around your ears.

It was late. Luke wanted to get back to the ranch. Share his news. Hold his soon-to-be son. Rid himself of the tensions of the day.

He looked at the sheet-draped figure on the bed. The decision was already made. There wasn't much of her to poke and prod. He hated hospitals himself. He couldn't abandon her in one.

"Does she need hospitalization?"

"Not really. A nurse just sponged her down and gave her some juice. She had no trouble drinking it. As long as she keeps up her fluid intake she'll be fine. She has no fever and there are no signs of any other infection. This medical card you found with her passport shows her shots are up-to-date. Unofficially I'd say all she needs is rest. If she has a place to go, someone to take care of her, we could release her. Otherwise I have to keep her here."

Luke swallowed, "I'll take full responsibility. I'm a relative."

So, God help him, he was. Of a kind.


Coming awake wasn't frightening. She was used to waking in strange places. A hut, a tent, the floor of a school. It was usually the attack on her senses that wakened her. Children screaming, a rooster crowing, the gabble of human voices that believed in operating at full lung capacity.

What alarmed Rachel now was she wasn't in a foreign, dirty, smelly, loud place, with the barest of amenities. Or in a foreign, clean, fragrant, quiet place, with the finest of luxuries. She'd been in both over the past few years.

She was in a four-poster bed. Large, luxurious, *frightening*. White priscilla drapes framed a piece of orange sky. Sunset? Sunrise?

Lily of the valley on a green background covered the walls. The sculptured carpet matched the background color of the elegant wallpaper perfectly. A cherry dresser gleamed against one wall. Outside someone was talking. Spanish. A woman laughed. The sound jogged Rachel's memory. This definitely wasn't the motel room she'd checked into. She turned her head.

A figure shot out of a chair in the corner. "She's awake. Come quick. She's awake." A well-built girl ran out of the room.

Rachel froze. Never had her waking up been a cause for rejoicing before. Was she hallucinating?

Boots rang on the wooden floor outside. The door was thrust wider. A man, backlit, stood there. Big. Wide. Blocking out the world. Fear receded as strength flowed out of him and wrapped her like velvet. The absurd sensations swamping her confirmed this had to be a dream.

"How are you feeling?"

Rachel thought about it for the first time since she'd woken up. She wiggled her toes, pinching herself surreptitiously under the bedclothes. Everything seemed to be in working condition. This was no dream. "Fine."

He came closer. It hit Rachel all at once. The telegram. The flight back. The courtroom scene. This wasn't the middle of someone else's nightmare. It was the middle of her own.

She'd lost Gordie. She'd never had him. Rachel closed her eyes. On top of the sheet one hand curled into a fist, highlighting white knuckles.

"Where does it hurt?" A hand was placed on hers. Warm, comforting, *protecting*.

Winner takes all. The last time she'd seen him he'd been swathed in victorious woman. His lawyer was obviously a woman of many talents.

"Where am I?"

She remembered the surge of current that had passed between them outside the courtroom. From him to her. At the time she hadn't paid much attention to it. She couldn't ignore it now. The big hand on hers ignited every nerve ending.

"At the Diamond Bar."

Rachel shot up in bed. Her head repaid her for the movement by swimming. Eyes closed, she willed herself better. Weakness was unaffordable.

"Your ranch. How did I get here?"

"I brought you here."

What was she? A brown paper parcel? The worst part was she had no recollection of any of it.

"How?" The squeak in her voice was denigrating. "I mean one minute I'm in my motel room, the next minute I wake up here...." She frowned.

Blanks weren't easy to fill. Besides, the tiny quivers of awareness that kept running through her interfered with concentration. Rachel hoped it was only malaria. It couldn't be this man. It shouldn't.

"I had to talk to you," Luke began slowly. She reminded him of a Chihuahua facing a grizzly. He had an idea she wasn't going to like what he'd done. "I followed you to the motel from the courthouse. You fainted. At the hospital the doctor said it was either staying there, or going to a place someone could take care of you. I brought you here."

He didn't miss the flicker of naked pain in her eyes. It tugged at his heartstrings. No one should be so alone.

It had been a fact so long, Rachel told herself, it shouldn't hurt. But she couldn't deny the aching mass of heaviness in her heart his words had raked over. The scar tissue wasn't as strong as she'd thought.

"How long have I been asleep?"

"A little over twenty-four hours. It's five in the evening now. The doctor at the hospital I took you to said you were suffering from exhaustion."

"You should have left me there," she said stubbornly, "Why didn't you?"

Navy blue eyes assessed her. Luke realized he couldn't tell her the truth. Not right now. She wouldn't tolerate any hint of compassion. He had yet to label the other feeling he was experiencing.

Luke opted for diplomacy. "I thought you might like to spend some time with Gordie, get to know him."

The name ripped her self-control. No. She didn't want to get to know the baby. Not now. Getting to know Gordie, then having to let go would break her. She couldn't risk it. There was only so much pain a heart could bear in one lifetime. So much aloneness.

Better a long-distance relationship, like the kind she'd had with Chris. Checks, letters, gifts from foreign locations. Impersonal, painless, *easy*. The kind Rachel Carstairs could handle like a professional.

The sound of the door opening dragged her back to the immediate present. An elderly woman bustled in. This had to be the housekeeper Luke had mentioned in court yesterday.

"There you are, awake at last!" A face beamed at her above a tray. Golden, love-warmed, it was framed in brown hair liberally sprinkled with white. Hazel eyes reflecting humor and happiness looked at her. Cheer and comfort exuded from every pore. Under her ample blue-and-white apron she wore a checked housedress. The accent reminded Rachel of the volunteer she'd met from Europe last year. "Welcome to the Diamond Bar. Slept twenty-hours straight you have. Did Luke tell you it's Saturday evening now? That was Angela, my niece by marriage, who was sitting with you. She's a good girl, just going through that emotional teenage stage when screaming is an accepted method of communication. Hope she didn't frighten you.''

Unspoken reassurance came across clearly with the information Hannah was giving her. *You're safe. We'll take good care of you.* "Luke brought you home because the doctor said all you needed was rest. No one can get that in a hospital . . . not the way they keep waking you up to check you *are* getting better. We were told to make sure you kept taking plenty of fluids and you did that all right. I guess it's time you ate something. Just brought you a light meal for now. We'll have dinner in a couple of hours.''

"This is Hannah who makes us all toe the line at the Diamond Bar,'' Luke said, affectionately introducing the woman who'd brought him up. "She helped put you to bed last night.''

Rachel touched her throat. She was in something voluminous and high-necked. *Safe.* Her hair was unbraided. The fingers she ran through it told her someone had brushed it for her. She would have to find something to tie it back with later. It was much too long to leave like this.

Turning to Hannah she held her hand out formally. "Thank you so much. I'm sorry to have been so much trouble.''

"No trouble at all, child.'' The gentle squeeze of Rachel's hand conveyed comfort and unlimited understanding. "It's a pleasure to have Christina's cousin here. She told me all about you. Kept saying how much she hoped you would come for a visit. Now don't you tire yourself out talking. Eat and rest or Luke here will bar me from this room. He calls me motor mouth as it is. I'll come back later and sponge you down. We'll catch up on everything once you're better.'' Hannah smiled, fluffed up her pillows and bustled out.

Rachel leaned back. The urge to burst into tears tightened the muscles in her throat to aching point. "I'm sorry to have made so much extra work."

Luke hooked his hands in his belt. "It's no trouble. Hannah loves having people around."

He didn't show any signs of leaving and Rachel slowly slid her legs out from under the white eyelet comforter. "I need to use—"

She never got the chance to finish the sentence. Strong arms swung her up to a strong chest. She was carried out the door, across the hall, into the bathroom and set on her feet. He kept an arm around her, till she found her balance.

"There's everything you might need in the top drawer." His breath stirred her hair. "I'll be right outside the door."

Five minutes later the process was repeated in reverse. Dazed, Rachel wondered if there was some rule about walking in this house that she wasn't aware of. Maybe they'd just shampooed their carpets and didn't want them dirtied. The echo of Luke's footsteps informed her of the error of her surmise. The corridors had wooden flooring.

In the minute it took to reach her room Rachel closed her eyes. It was the only way to shut him out. Even so the picture of his firm chin, the slash of his nose, the warmth of his gaze, was branded on her mind. Three of her other senses ran amok. He smelled of the outdoors, of smoke, of hard work. He felt like rock under the softness of a much washed, checked shirt. He sounded like the rush of water over a gravel bed. She heard something about the doctor ordering complete rest.

"I can walk," Rachel protested.

It didn't sound like her at all. Shy, breathless, *flustered*. Where was all the self-possession of the past few years? She'd worked with and treated men of all ages. There was no reason for this one to affect her like this.

She tried again. "I'm perfectly all right."

"Not till the doctor says so." Her words could have just been so much water off a duck's back. "I'm taking you in to see Dr. Kenton tomorrow, for some tests. He's the family doctor. Till then you're to stay put."

Placing her on the bed, he gently spread her hair over the pillow. Tucking her in as if she were an errant child, he anchored her with an oak bed tray. "Eat."

Rachel stared at the tray. There was enough food to last her three days. Oven warm croissants, freshly curled pats of butter, three varieties of jam. Under a covered dish rested two poached eggs. A glass of freshly squeezed juice caught her eye. If this was a *light* meal she would need help when dinnertime came around.

She sipped at the juice. As soon as he left she would take the tray back to the kitchen and explain to Hannah that she couldn't possibly eat all this food.

But Luke had no intention of leaving. He pulled a chair up to the bed, straddled it. After a while he took the glass of juice out of her hand and repeated, "Eat."

He wasn't going to mind his own business. Resignedly she broke off a piece of the croissant and chewed on it. Immediately her salivary glands came to life, begging for more.

As Luke watched her a throbbing began in his jaw. One might think she had reconstituted shoe leather in her mouth. Reaching forward he picked up a croissant, slathered it with butter, topped it off with peach and apricot jelly and held it out to her.

Her eyes widened but she took it from him. The fingers that brushed his were icy cold. Luke's eyes fixed on the stain of color in her cheekbones. He wanted to pick up the chair and hurl it out of the window.

What was wrong with the woman? No one could be that self-controlled. He'd expected questions, an argument, a protest at the very least. Not docile acceptance of every-thing he said and did. What made Rachel Carstairs wrap herself in lead-lined layers of indifference? The answer would provide him with the key to understanding her.

Halfway through the croissant she gave up. He didn't push it.

"Want something else?"

"Can I have some coffee?"

"Sorry. The doctor said no caffeine." He hadn't, but Luke knew it wouldn't do her any good. "Would you like some herbal tea? Hannah swears by it."

"No thank you."

He lifted the tray. Rachel sank back on the mound of pil-lows and closed her eyes. It was as good a dismissal as any she could think of.

Behind the screen of closed lids her thoughts rioted. Why had Luke Summers brought her here? The sooner she was out of this bed and back in LA the better.

"What has she been living on?" Hannah asked fiercely as he entered the kitchen with the tray. "I've seen starving cattle look better."

Hannah knew more about Rachel than he did. In fact, it was she who'd filled him in with a few details of Chris's cousin before the case. Apparently his sister-in-law had talked about Rachel to the rest of the family.

"It's a long flight from Bangladesh," Luke explained, puzzled by the unusual urge to protect her. "I talked to Jenks, her lawyer, this morning. According to him, she came straight to the courthouse from the airport. From the time she left the village she was working in, to the time she got off the plane at LAX she'd been traveling for seventy-two hours straight. Engine trouble in Hong Kong held the flight up twelve hours. She's been under a terrific strain, not knowing if she would get here on time. Add jet lag to that and it's going to take her a while to get back to normal."

"Wonder why she wanted Gordie?" Hannah muttered to herself. "If she's after the money, I'm the reincarnation of Marilyn Monroe." There was a silence while she watched Luke eat the poached eggs. "Did she ask to see Gordie?"

"She's still very tired." Why was he defending her? He'd thought it strange himself that she hadn't shown any interest in the child.

"Hmph." Hannah wasn't to be fooled. "Something's very wrong here. And if you tell me I'm imagining things, Luke Summers, I'm going to be mad enough to serve up boiled carrots for dinner."

But Luke had no answer for her. Snatching Gordie from his playpen he swung him high till the room was filled with childish chuckles. Setting his nephew on his shoulders, he strode from the room.

It didn't matter if Rachel Carstairs wasn't interested in getting to know Gordie. The baby would never lack for love on the Diamond Bar. Half the ranch hands had hung around till he'd gotten home last night. Their victory yell at the news he'd won had been uproarious. Quite a few of them had grown up with him and Rob. They shared his love and pride in Gordie.

The fact that he'd brought the opposition home with him had subdued them. Interest had been rife as they'd watched him carry the limp form into the house. But they knew better than to question his actions.

Hannah had barely brought one of her nightdresses to the guest room when Gordon had started crying. Luke had slipped away to check on him, and by the time he'd returned their involuntary guest had been settled for the night.

The decision to sleep in her room had been automatic. Hannah's days were filled with watching the baby. He couldn't ask her to work a night shift as well. Neither could he leave Rachel Carstairs alone in the guest wing of the house. She might wake disoriented and terrified. He settled matters by taking the baby monitor with him to the guest room. If Gordie cried he would be in his room before his nephew had drawn his second breath.

She was a restless sleeper. Her tossing had the quilt on the floor twice. The first time he retrieved it he'd made a discovery. She slept on her stomach. Muttered words in a foreign language snapped him back to attention. Tucking the quilt around her he returned to his sleeping bag.

The short scream a few minutes later had him on his feet before he could place it.

"Tom, hurry, please. The woman. I can't hold on much longer. Tom."

She was thrashing madly, her unseeing eyes wide open, her arms straining to hold some unknown body. Her thin wail of despair whipped through him like a northerly. Luke gathered her to his chest.

"Hush," he scolded. "You're home now. There's nothing to worry about."

She stilled so suddenly he thought she'd slid back into sleep. But she hadn't.

"Home?" The eyes were focusing now. "I'm home?"

Emotion tore at his throat. There was a bank of yearning in the gray eyes so close to his own. A bank of disbelief. The desire to change that look shook Luke to the core of his being.

"Yes."

She pressed against him. Her eyelids drooped but her words were crystal clear, "Don't ever let me go."

She lifted her hands, following the lines of his body from his hands to his shoulders, up his cheeks, then into his hair. She brought his head down to hers, still searching for the promise he'd offered. Her eyes remained closed in an effort to preserve the mirage. The lips that touched his were as soft as rose petals.

The contact changed everything. Suddenly her grip tightened as if she were searching desperately for some sort of proof. Luke kissed her back as he would a child, wanting to give her the reassurance she so badly needed. He wasn't sure when passion took over. Only that he was drowning in the sweetness of her mouth and she was trying to pull him down with her.

"Please," she pleaded in that raspy voice of hers, "please hold me."

Her tone cut the cord of desire. Rachel Carstairs was ill. She didn't know what was she was doing or saying. This was as far as her dream could go.

"Hush," he ordered again, hauling air into his lungs, as he held her head against his chest. "Just go back to sleep."

He rocked her as if she were a baby, waiting for her to calm down. When he finally laid her back on the pillows, she had a half smile on her face. For the first time since he'd seen her, Rachel Carstairs looked at peace.

An awesome fierceness welled up in him. Strong, protective, *overwhelming*. He tried to shake it off. Impulses had no room in a practical man's thoughts.

Checking to see if she had a fever, brushing a stray tendril off her face, tucking her in again, had all been done automatically. He'd returned to his sleeping bag but not to sleep.

Luke looked at Gordie on the rug of his study. His nephew had managed to haul himself to his feet, holding onto the seat of a chair. Round navy eyes scanned the area for anything more interesting than mere toys. Luke handed him a ball. It was brushed aside.

Rachel Carstairs was an enigma. He couldn't rest till he knew why she'd wanted Gordie, as well as why she didn't even want to see the baby now. Luke had an idea that the answers would be hard to come by. She wasn't going to help.

He checked on her at dinnertime but she was fast asleep. Tucking the bedclothes around her, he paused and placed a hand against her cheek. Amazingly enough, her skin was soft and creamy. Luke thought of the picture he'd had of a leathery ogre and a corner of his mouth tilted up. So much for misconceptions.

He remembered Chris mentioning once that her cousin had joined MRA right after high school. Luke wondered what had motivated Rachel to alienate herself from everything that was familiar.

# Chapter Three

Rachel awoke before dawn. It took a few minutes for her mind to marshal her thoughts into order. Luke had brought her here Friday night. She'd met Hannah Saturday evening. Sunday was a vague blur of resting, being sponged down, changed and having her hair brushed gently. Everytime she opened her eyes she'd been coaxed to eat or drink something. Once she had woken to find Luke by the window, his back to her. Maybe drifting in and out of sleep for most of the day had been self-defense.

Someone had thoughtfully placed a clock on her nightstand. Luminescent hands pointed to four o'clock. The light told her dawn wasn't far away. It was now Monday morning. It was cold. So cold. She needed to use the bathroom. Quiet as a summer breeze she crept from the room.

Rachel's gaze passed over the pretty wallpaper, the marble washbasin, the gilt-edged mirror, the lush plants in the enormous bathroom and settled on the bathtub. Sunk into the floor, the perfect green oval tub beckoned like an oasis in the desert. Irresistible.

A quick survey showed no other closed doors in the corridor. If she didn't turn on the taps full blast she really shouldn't disturb anyone.

It felt so good to slide into the hot water. Her muscles shivered at first contact with the balmy warmth and then relaxed. The scent of lavender rose soothingly with the steam. Hoping fleetingly no one would mind her lavish use of bath oil and crystals, Rachel slid deeper into the water and sighed with satisfaction. Heaven should be so nice.

Luke waited a while. After five minutes the sleeping bag he'd used the last two nights on the floor of her room seemed too confining. What if she'd fainted in there? Dr. Andrews had been very explicit about her condition. Sliding out of the sleeping bag he got to his feet.

He tapped on the door of the bathroom. Once, twice. There was no answer.

"Rachel?"

He heard a small splash and realized what he'd interrupted. The faint music he could identify as country stopped as she switched off the little radio in the bathroom. Luke opened his mouth to apologize and explain.

"Yes?"

Her voice from just behind the door sounded anxious. Luke wondered what it was about him that produced this reaction. Could a recollection of what had passed between them her first night here be the reason for her uneasiness around him?

"I was just checking on you. I thought maybe you weren't feeling well again."

Guilt laced her next words heavily. "I'm sorry if I woke you. There were no other doors. I thought it would be okay...."

"Don't stay in there too long," Luke ordered softly. "You might catch cold."

Resisting the impulse to snatch her up when she came out and carry her back to her bed as if she were Gordie's age was hard.

"I'm almost done."

The retreating footsteps told her he'd gone back to bed. Taking her mood with him. Toweling herself dry, Rachel used a washcloth to clean the sides of the tub.

Jet lag. That was it. It did strange things to people. It accounted for why she felt so jumpy whenever Luke Summers was around.

Rinsing the washcloth she spread it on a rack to dry. Dropping the towel Rachel looked around for her nightdress. Her reflection in the mirror above the washbasin claimed her attention. Wiping the steam away, Rachel looked at her body with a kind of detached curiosity. The last time she'd seen herself full-length had been in a river. The murkiness had been kind. This clear glass wasn't. She examined the hollows of her neck, the skinny body. Nothing there to write home about.

Hesitating a moment, she reached for the talc. Might as well go the whole bit. Where she was going, it would be a while before she could indulge herself like this again.

Sheer surprise halted her in the doorway of her room. The lamp beside her bed threw a golden glow on the sleeping bag on the floor, the man in it. Rachel gaped at the picture he presented. Tousled hair, sleep laden eyes and a wickedly delicious chest. Luke Summers was playing Florence Nightingale.

"You don't have to sleep in here," she said stiffly. "I'm fine." He must be uncomfortable sleeping in his jeans.

The quivers running up and down her spine had to be malaria. It had been a rotten idea to bathe at this hour.

Rachel's gaze got tangled up in the nest of hair on Luke's chest. Speech got tangled up somewhere deep inside.

"That's okay." The way he dismissed sleeping on the ground reminded her of the scene in court. He had minimized everything he'd done for Gordie, as well. "I'm perfectly fine now, so you don't have to sleep here anymore."

In her line of work she'd seen plenty of naked torsos. Of every size, shape and color. None of them had made her want to sink out of sight or wish for the vital statistics of a beauty pageant contestant.

"It's four-thirty now." His tone held calm quiet reason. "Hannah's a very light sleeper. Going back to my room will wake her and she won't be able to go back to sleep."

There was nothing more to say. Rachel got into bed quietly hoping he didn't have the same problem as Hannah.

"Would you like some warm milk?"

Her eyes landed on the tray on the nightstand. A mug and two pieces of toast nestled on a white embroidered cloth.

"Please." The tears weren't far away. "You don't have to do all this." No one ever had before. A starved heart was likely to blow it out of all proportion.

"Try the milk. It will help you sleep."

She mightn't have spoken at all. He was doing his bulldozer bit again.

Rachel tried to get through to him again. "I'm fine. One hundred percent fit. Tomorrow when we go into town I'll catch a bus back to LA. I have to let someone at MRA know where I am."

That was it? She was just going to up and leave? Shock made him sit up, speak his thoughts aloud. "What about Gordie?"

For a while she was so quiet he thought she hadn't heard. But she had. Her voice when she answered him wasn't quite even. It held the raspy edge he'd heard before. "I'm sure you and the Diamond Bar are what's best for him."

"Don't you even want to see him?"

Rachel struggled with herself. The negative answer trembled on her lips, but she didn't let it out. Always sensitive to emotion, she could almost put her hand out and touch Luke's leashed anger now. He had every right to be exasperated. First she took him to court for the child, and then she acted as if she didn't even want to see Chris's son.

Rachel bit her lip. "I'll see him in the morning."

Something didn't add up right. Luke asked himself why Rachel Carstairs was no longer interested in Gordie. It was too quick a switch to make sense. Hauling a deep breath of air into his lungs he let it out slowly. Trying to understand her was like trying to gather a fistful of cobwebs.

In the few seconds she'd stood in the doorway he was reminded of a child playacting again. The scent of lavender had teased his nostrils and her eyes had looked like tar pits. He hadn't missed the quiver of her lips or the way she'd sidled past the sleeping bag. Hannah's baggy gown was much too large for her, which wasn't surprising since the housekeeper was at least a hundred pounds heavier. The scrubbed shiny look brought to mind the littlest angel in a recent television show. With a halo that was definitely askew.

"Don't you want to spend a while here, get to know Gordie?"

Hannah's oft spoken, stern reminder to him and Rob all through their teens came to mind. *A gentleman didn't pester a lady.* Only he wasn't ready to be gentlemanly about this. There was something unreal about Rachel Carstairs. Something that got past his veneer of civilization and touched a primitive core he hadn't known existed.

"No." The treble intensified, the knuckles showed white against the mug.

"Why not?"

She had to say something to shut him up. Once and for all. Truth popped out. "It'll be easier this way."

So, that was it. Rachel Carstairs didn't want to risk getting attached to Gordie. But why? The judge's decision had freed her to pursue the work she loved *and* visit Gordie as often as she liked. Unless . . . Luke wondered if she'd decided half a loaf was no good. If she couldn't have it all she wanted nothing. He frowned. No, he didn't think that was it. There had been that odd rasp in her voice again, the sound that he was beginning to recognize as a sign of stress. The only other explanation was that Rachel was afraid of getting involved with the child now. Afraid of loving.

She put her mug back on the tray, wiped her milk moustache off with the back of her hand, slipped back into bed and switched off the light. Luke lay back and laced his fingers under his head.

In half an hour the house would come to life. Gordie always woke at six. It was usually his chirrups that started Luke's day. They shared the first half hour of the day together. Right after his first bottle Gordie was at his best.

If anyone had told Luke six months ago that a baby's gurgling and cooing could make such a difference he would have thought them insane. Now it was the only way to start the day.

No vice presidency could ever take precedence over his soon-to-be son. The child represented his brother's dreams. A sacred trust. Anything else came second. The ranch was the best place for the boy to grow up. A child needed fresh air, open spaces. There had been no regret, no futile reluctance. Making decisions had always been easy for him. Until now. Until Rachel Carstairs.

He could let her go the way she wanted to. But inside him was this deep, powerful tide of feeling that told him he wasn't going to be so amenable.

Luke sighed and looked over in her direction. He could barely make her out. She was a mere slice in that big bed. As usual her stillness bothered him. It was as if she felt that by being quiet the world would pass her by instead of picking on her. Somewhere along the line, Rachel had to have suffered badly. He intended to do something about it.

"Penny for them?"

He knew she was awake. Never any good at pretense, Rachel cleared her throat. What she had to say needed camouflage. Dawn offered gentle encouragement, lighting outlines not details. Her face was always a dead giveaway.

"I'll leave an address where you can reach me. If ever anything happens to change your mind about Gordie, let me know." She was proud of her voice. Impersonal, cool, brisk. "In town tomorrow I'll open a joint account in all three of our names and transfer my money into it. It's not much, but please don't hesitate to use it for Gordie. From time to time I'll send more." She could have done without that betraying wobble at the end, but at least it was said.

What on earth was the woman talking about? Luke thought.

She was talking as if she never expected to see any of them again. As if it didn't matter to her. Was her other life so important? Was this Tom fellow waiting for her back there?

"Tell me about your work."

Relief he wasn't going to argue about her decision washed over Rachel. "I'm part of a medical relief team that just goes wherever we're needed."

"How many people are there in this team?"

"Two doctors, two nurses, two aides."

"How many countries have you worked in?"

"I've spent all my time in Bangladesh, in different villages."

"What kind of work do you do there?"

"We have a field clinic that's open twenty-four hours, more or less. In addition, we try to teach the people a few basic facts about health and hygiene."

She didn't tell him that at times they were all doctors. Rachel had incised sores, stitched wounds, even pulled out teeth. When you were all there was between life and suffering, you did anything and everything.

"You must like your work very much. You've been with MRA five years now. Most people do what? A two-year stint?"

"One year. I've only been there four and a half years, not five. Dr. Tom Atwell, my boss, has been with MRA since its inception in the early seventies."

Her boss. Not her lover. Rachel's tone would have told him if he was.

"Don't you ever want to come home for good?"

Home? There had never been a place that fit that description. Not in her entire life. In the barren emptiness of her life from the age of ten to eighteen there had been one bright spot. The summer she'd spent with her father's sister in Wisconsin. Mary Jennings had wanted to adopt her but her father had refused angrily. During that one summer on the dairy farm Rachel had known love. Aunt Mary's daughter, Christina, a year older than her, had offered her both friendship and love, and a starved Rachel had collected every crumb and stored it to make up for all the years she'd gone without.

Christina had been generous. She'd shared her parents, her pets, her clothes, without any reservations. In the sunshine of Chris's easygoing nature, Rachel had blossomed, learned to laugh, even put on a little weight. They had sworn to be sisters forever. They'd never met again. Letters had been their only link.

Rachel's father had died when she was nineteen, soon after the first anniversary of her arrival in Bangladesh. A massive heart attack, Christina had written Rachel. A neighbor had called the police, alarmed by his dog's frantic barking at Les Carstairs's door. The police had found him dead and contacted his sister whose name and address they'd located by the telephone.

Rachel had cried when she'd heard the news; for a man who hadn't known how to be a father; for what might have been. She'd waited for more news, clinging to the hope that he would have left a letter for her telling her what he couldn't during his lifetime. That he had indeed cared for her.

But happy endings, Rachel had once again had to acknowledge, belonged only in fiction. Aunt Mary had written that all his things had been disposed of. There had been no personal effects worth keeping. She didn't even think of the money her father had left her as hers. It was no substitute for the love she'd craved.

Chris had kept in touch. Twice a year Rachel had received long gossipy letters about Chris's secretarial classes, the men in her life. She'd moved to California after her mother's death and taken up a job at the University of California, Santa Barbara. Time and again she would ask Rachel to return. They would share a flat. Rachel could take some classes, maybe even get a job at the university. The letters always ended the same way. Tons of love and kisses. Intangible love.

Rachel hadn't been able to put her thoughts into words. Her briefly scrawled postcards kept communication open but the door to her real feelings closed. She was afraid to risk failing in a one-on-one relationship again.

Then Chris had met Rob Summers. He'd come to the university for some forms for the daughter of a friend. It had been love at first sight.

After she was married, Chris's letters had become more insistent. She wanted Rachel to come and spend a vacation at the ranch, get to know her new family. They were wonderful people. Rachel would love them. Rachel had chosen not to try and find out.

Lost in her own thoughts she forgot Luke had asked her a question.

What had he said now to send her back into her shell? Hannah and the doctor were both right. She was a mass of nerves.

"Rachel?" Propping himself on an elbow, Luke wondered if she hadn't fallen asleep again.

"I'm sorry. What did you say?"

"Don't you ever want to come home for good?"

"There's nothing for me here now."

The stark statement was like a knife in his gut. Questions bombarded his brain but he didn't let them out. Getting to know Rachel Carstairs, coaxing her trust, couldn't be accomplished in one talk. It would take more than a knight in shining armor to solve this particular riddle. It was suddenly of paramount importance that he should do so as quickly as possible. Luke lay back, linking his fingers under his head. Any successful campaign needed a plan.

Gordie sucked on his first bottle of the day with vigor. Changed and freshly talcumed he smelled like rain-washed flowers. His skin felt like crushed silk. Dark eyes, exactly like Luke's, were fixed on his uncle's face. From time to time a hand came up and patted one cheek. Sturdy legs flailed the air. He was in a hurry to be done, to get on with the day.

"Easy champ, easy," Luke coaxed. "You're going to get sick if you drink it down so fast."

Gordie didn't alter his pace and a few minutes later Luke put his nephew on his shoulder, patting him till he burped. Once, twice.

A sound in the kitchen doorway alerted him to Rachel's presence. She was wearing the skirt of her pink suit with a sleeveless blouse. She looked chilled.

The sunshine feigned warmth but the outdoor thermometer read forty-two. December mornings could be very cold here.

Rachel's smile became strained as her eyes settled on Gordie. For a moment there was a flash of intensity that blinded. Then her mask slid back in place.

"Gordie," Luke turned the baby to face her, "Meet your aunt."

He'd decided Gordie would do his bit. Rachel needed to belong. A second cousin sounded like a distant relationship; calling her an aunt would make her feel more like part of the family.

Gordie looked at her for several seconds and then burrowed his head in Luke's neck. He was beginning to recognize faces.

"He's so cute." Rachel turned away. She might have been discussing the weather. Only the rasp in her voice betrayed her.

Hannah bustled in and Rachel returned her greeting with warmth. Yes, she felt perfectly fine now, thank you. No, she couldn't stay in bed any longer. "May I help with breakfast?"

The older woman recognized the stamp of strain on Rachel's face for what it was immediately. She heard the plea behind the words. Rearing two boys had given her emotional radar. Over the baby's red-gold curls, Hannah transmitted a silent message to Luke: *Don't rush her.*

"Of course," she said warmly. "Set the table for me will you, Rachel? The plates are in the cabinet by the dishwasher and the cutlery's in the drawer above it."

Breakfast seemed a feast at the Diamond Bar. Steaming oatmeal, jugs of cream, a pile of pancakes, curls of yellow butter, maple syrup, a covered dish of sausage and eggs.

Rachel sipped at her juice, making no move to eat. She'd thought she had fortified herself mentally to be detached about Chris's son. The giant leap of love her heart had given at her first sight of him told her she hadn't gotten near enough to success.

"Hannah, thank you for everything." Rachel cleared her throat, felt Luke's dark eyes on her. "I'm sorry I made so much work for you."

Hannah's answering look was a question.

"Rachel wants to get back to LA today," Luke explained noncommittally.

"Where's the fire?" There was no mistaking Hannah's amazement. For once her smile had vanished completely and her hazel eyes seemed flecked with question marks. "You've just gotten here. You don't look well enough to go back to all that smog."

"Rachel has to let someone at MRA headquarters know where she is. She'll probably be leaving for Bangladesh tomorrow," Luke supplied smoothly.

He flashed a warning and Hannah nodded in perfect understanding. "Send us a postcard will you?"

Luke's compliance shouldn't grate. It was what she wanted, wasn't it? Rachel knew the sooner she got back on the job the quicker she could revert to normal. She didn't belong here. It was silly to feel reluctant to leave, to let her-

self think she was anything but a transient here was dangerous.

"Eat," Luke ordered.

"I'm not hungry." Even the juice couldn't trickle down
any more. "In fact, if I could catch an earlier bus back to
LA I could see a doctor there and save you some time."

Luke thought of the stack of papers waiting for him, of
the urgent message on his computer to contact the head office, of gray eyes wrapped in hurt.

"I have nothing to do today. You're not leaving until Dr.
Kenton sees you. Now eat." He ladled oatmeal into a bowl
and placed it in front of her.

Rachel picked up her spoon. The oatmeal was a surprise.
Fat juicy raisins and crunchy almonds were hidden in it. The
first spoonful hit a spot that clamored for more.

Luke was saying something about a fence to Hannah.
Rachel's eyes slid to Gordie. He was busy with the things on
the bar that straddled his exercise mat. His victory cry as he
managed to grasp one of the plastic rings was followed by a
flood of baby talk. Rachel's heart melted. He was a darling.

"That wasn't so bad was it?" Luke sounded gruff, as he
had in court.

She looked at her bowl. It was empty.

Luke worked his way through a stack of pancakes in silence. He'd fielded the look that had rested on Gordie. Naked yearning. Why was Rachel hiding what she felt for the
child? She wasn't leaving here till he found out what was
behind her charade.

"Hannah, if you would show Rachel around outside, I
have a phone call to make before we leave for Santa Barbara. I'll get a jacket for her."

He was back in a minute with a blue windcheater. "Angela always keeps a spare jacket here. This will fit you better than any of mine."

Ignoring her outstretched hand he held it for her. When she had her arms in place, he turned her around and began to button it up. Heat coursed through Rachel, showing in her face.

"I can do that."

If she stayed around any longer she would begin to be the helpless creature this man thought her.

"I know." The fierce look was back in his eyes. Rachel wondered how she'd offended him. He reached the top button, looked at her, then brushed a strand of hair off her forehead, as if he couldn't help himself.

A veranda and three wide steps separated the ranch house from a green lawn that meandered out of sight. On every side rolling hills undulated. Rachel could see a few cattle on a distant slope.

"I'm sure Chris told you we're tucked into the Santa Ynez mountain range. Behind that hill—" Hannah pointed to the row of Italian Cypress that screened the house on one side "—is the farm. Near it are the ranch hands' quarters and a couple of cottages. The other staff quarters, we call them help houses here, are spread out throughout the ranch. The one closest to us is the farm manager's. Juan Rodriguez, the manager, is my brother-in-law. Theresa, whom you met yesterday, is his wife and Angela's their daughter. Marie, who helps in the house, is a cousin's daughter. I married Juan's older brother, Carlos, when I was eighteen. Carlos died five years ago when a horse threw him. Since then I lived in one of the smaller cottages, semi-retired, till the accident last July.

Rachel didn't need to be told that Hannah's giving up of her retirement had been voluntary. She wouldn't delegate the task of caring for Rob's son to anybody else.

"You've been here a long time."

"Yes. I came out from Denmark when I was fifteen to live with my married sister in Solvang. Two years later I saw the advertisement for a cook at the Diamond Bar in the local paper and applied for the job. I didn't know a thing about American cooking, but I learned. I met Carlos soon after I came here. Our only regret in the fifty-two years we were married was that we had no children of our own. Rob and Luke made up for it though."

Moisture seeped into Hannah's eyes as she stared into the distance.

"Luke's father lives in Arizona now," Hannah continued after a while. "He's been here four times since the accident, even offered to move back if it would help, but Luke won't let him. His arthritis almost cripples him when he's here. Luke's convinced him we have it all under control. He hired Angela and Marie to help in the house, so I can have all my time free for Gordie. I still like to do the cooking though."

Rachel stared out at the hills wreathed in lazy mists. What strange law made one man such a wonderful father, another a total failure? She'd watched the way Luke picked up the baby, held him, tended to his needs. There was no awkwardness there. His hugs and kisses were an open declaration about how he felt about his nephew. Of one thing there could be no doubt—Gordie wouldn't ever lack for love here. The fact that she would never see Chris's son again shouldn't matter.

"Ready?" Luke's gaze skimmed Rachel's face, took in the corralled tears. He'd come up so quietly behind them she hadn't even heard him.

She was as ready as she would ever be. Luke was carrying her handbag and her rucksack. She hadn't even remembered them. What was the sign she'd seen in railway carriages in India? *Less luggage, more comfort. Make travel a pleasure.* She certainly qualified as their official mascot. No excess baggage. Material or emotional.

"I need to..." It was the only excuse she could think of to go in once again.

Luke nodded. "I'll wait right here."

Gordie was in his playpen. On her way back from the bathroom, she paused a microsecond by him. Hannah was in the walk-in pantry with her back to her. Rachel leaned down and kissed the baby on the cheek. She was entitled to one memory.

"Gaga," Gordie said agreeably.

"Love you," whispered Rachel.

To Rachel's relief, Luke didn't seem to notice her tension as they drove away from the ranch in a blue pickup truck. He talked about the ranch, how his great grandfather had come west in a wagon train during the gold rush.

"He didn't find any gold, but the land and the climate kept him here. He staked out five-hundred acres. He refused to grow grapes, though. He ran cattle and horses."

Rachel had been staring out of her window since they left the ranch. Her usual stony shuttered look was back in place. So, thought Luke with satisfaction, leaving Gordie is costing her. He needed to be sure.

"Great Grandpa Jasper had only one son, Robert," he continued smoothly, "Grandpa Rob had three children, two daughters and one son—my father, Gordon. Both my aunts went to colleges back east. One is married to a farmer in Virginia, the other is in Australia. Mom was a neighboring rancher's daughter. She said she decided to marry Dad when she was ten. It took him ten years after that, though, to get around to proposing to her. Mom was crazy about Thoroughbreds. Soon after they were married she and Dad worked on a proposal to make the Diamond Bar a breeding and training farm and presented it to Grandpa Gordon with quivering knees. Grandpa took one look at it and said anyone who'd put so much thought into it as to write a fifty-page report deserved a chance. He lived long enough to see the Diamond Bar well on its way to becoming one of the finest Thoroughbred ranches in the state.''

Dr. Kenton's office was right on the outskirts of town. A nurse took Rachel away for tests a few minutes after they arrived. Then Dr. Kenton examined her. By the time she dressed again and went into his office, he and Luke were chatting pleasantly.

"Ms. Carstairs, the news isn't bad." The older man smiled reassuringly across the table. With his white hair and tanned skin he looked more like a prosperous rancher than a doctor. "It isn't too good, either."

"What's wrong?" She'd always taken her health for granted.

"Have you been ill recently?"

Rachel thought back. "I had a bout with amoebic dysentery in the summer but I got over it quickly."

Dr. Kenton frowned at the charts on his desk. "Well, apparently your body doesn't agree. Your hemoglobin count is very low. You're not well enough to go back to Bangladesh."

"Not well enough...." Rachel stared at the elderly man in disbelief. "There has to be some mistake."

"I'm afraid not. You need rest, relaxation and more rest. I'm going to prescribe a vitamin and iron supplement. If we find anything else out from the rest of your lab work, we'll be in touch. Otherwise I'd like you to take things real easy and report back here in a fortnight. With your background, I'm sure I don't have to go over iron rich foods with you. Include plenty of them in your diet."

They were on the road back to the ranch before Rachel realized the direction they were headed. A sign for Mrs. Kelly's Teas confirmed it. She'd noticed it on the way out.

"Why are we going back to the ranch?" If her memory served right the sign was some sort of halfway point. Well, this was one time Luke Summers wouldn't get his own way. He had to turn around even if it took him the rest of the day to get home.

He hadn't said much since they'd left the doctor's office. Now he looked at her briefly. "You heard what the doctor said. You need rest and relaxation."

"I can rest in LA."

The diagnosis had surprised her. MRA always insisted on frequent, thorough check-ups. With all that had been going on in Bangladesh the past couple of months Tom hadn't even mentioned the usual physical, but in September he'd told her everything was normal.

"In a motel room?" Luke's tone told her what he thought of those. A vision of yellow cabbage roses on a brown-and-green background came to mind and Rachel knew she wasn't very keen on the idea herself. "Your lungs need fresh air, not smog."

"MRA has a hostel I can stay in."

"Hannah wouldn't forgive me if I let you go in this condition."

"I can't impose on you any longer."

He didn't answer.

Duty, thought Rachel. He thinks it's his duty to take me back to the ranch.

"Luke I have to get to LA today." Getting away was imperative.

"Why?" he asked reasonably. "There's no way you can go back abroad right away. The Diamond Bar is as good a place to convalesce as any."

"I can't go back."

"You can."

He didn't know a thing. This big man seemed to think life came in orderly little packets marked simple and happy.

"No.'

"Yes."

Rachel bit her lip and stared out of the window in frustration. She couldn't afford to lose her temper with him now. There was too much at stake. Rapidly her brain searched for the best approach to take. Stubborn men had to be coaxed not prodded. How on earth did one do that?

"Whatever you're afraid of, has to be faced." Rachel couldn't believe she was hearing the words. "It's the only way."

Inexplicably, moisture seeped into her eyes. He *knew* she was running away? With the exception of Christina, no one had ever been able to tell what was going on inside her mind. No one had cared enough to try.

Luke Summers made life sound so easy. Maybe he was right. Maybe it was time to gather her courage for one more shot at happiness.

A part of Rachel's heart, covered for years with thick layers of rejection, opened and a frail shoot of hope took root. She looked at the hills. The mists had vanished. Sunshine caressed the slopes like an omen.

# Chapter Four

The next instant Rachel knew she couldn't let herself be fooled by kindness. That's all she was being offered. Translating hospitality and compassion into anything else was opening the door to trouble. "Just for a day or two," she ceded. Sometimes one had to surrender a battle to win a war.

"Yes."

"I need a change of clothes." The pink suit had been cleaned and pressed but she couldn't wear it indefinitely.

If they'd had this discussion sooner she could have bought a few things in town. Now it was too late.

The jerk of Luke's head directed her to the back of the pickup. Rachel's eyes widened at the sight of two plastic bags next to the brown grocery bags. The name of a well-known department store leaped out at her. He'd gone shopping for her? An unexpected tremulous warmth flared in the pit of Rachel's stomach.

"I bought you a few things." There was nothing in his tone that implied it was anything more than just another detail he'd seen to. "The rest you can order through catalogs. When you're better we'll go down to LA, for a real shopping spree."

Rachel's breath stuck halfway in her windpipe. *When you're better. Real shopping spree.* His words insinuated more than she could handle. Permanence, forever, *always.* That was impossible. She had to remember her stay at the Diamond Bar was a temporary thing, the whim of a stubborn man. To imagine anything else would be weak and Rachel always stamped out all weaknesses before they germinated. Life was less complicated that way.

A few days at the Diamond Bar and then she would leave.

Hannah was overjoyed to have her back. "We'll take good care of you," she promised, her smile making her eyes almost disappear. "In no time you'll be as fit as a fiddle."

Smiling weakly Rachel refused an offer of tea and a Danish. "If you don't mind, I'll go to my room for a while." She needed to sort her thoughts out.

"Of course," Hannah said briskly. "The drive has worn you out."

Luke took a step forward and Rachel moved back quickly, afraid he was going to carry her there.

His eyes glinted as he read her expression correctly. "Let me show you to your room."

"I know the way to my room." Had the doctor told him something else about her that she didn't know?

"That's the guest room." Luke's warm hand cupped her elbow and steered her in the opposite direction. "You'll be more comfortable in this one."

She couldn't remember walking down the hallway or entering the big, bright room. All she was conscious of was heat pouring into her veins, the point of entry, her elbow.

"I'm perfectly fine where I am."

"Jason uses the guest room when I'm not here," Luke continued as if she hadn't spoken. "Sometimes Angela spends the night with us. This room has a telephone, your own television set, an attached bathroom and a nicer view."

It also had closets the size of a jumbo jet. "Thank you."

Luke nodded. "Make yourself at home. Ask Hannah for anything you need. Someone or other goes into town every day. All you have to do is give Hannah a list of what you want and it'll be here the same day."

"Thank you." The chorus sounded monotonous even to Rachel but there was nothing else she could say. Luke was like a powerful current. One she didn't have the strength to fight.

"Have a small nap before lunch," he suggested. "Marie will bring you a tray here. Another day in bed won't hurt."

He was gone before Rachel could open her mouth to let him know she was perfectly all right.

Her packages had already been placed there by Marie. The bags yielded six sets of underwear in pastel colors, two pairs of jeans, a wraparound skirt, four tops, two night-dresses, a robe, two sweaters and a warm jacket. More clothes than she'd bought herself at one time. Ever. Rachel tried on a pair of jeans and a sweater. Another bag she hadn't noticed earlier had a pair of gym shoes and a pair of house slippers in it. At the bottom of the bag she found one of the pair of house slippers Hannah had lent her. The housekeeper had jokingly mentioned the only thing they seemed to have in common physically was the size of their feet.

To have taken Hannah's slipper along, Luke had to have been very sure she was coming back. And he'd done the shopping even before she'd gotten the test results from Dr. Kenton. How could he possibly have known what the doctor was going to tell her? Unless...? Rachel shook her head. No. She wasn't that important to Luke, that he might try to trick her into staying on. And Dr. Kenton wouldn't falsify a report.

"Shall I hang up the things for you?" Rachel looked up as Marie came in with a glass of juice.

"No, thanks." Horrified that Marie might think she expected to be waited on Rachel said quickly, "I'll do it. I have nothing else to do anyway."

Rachel's gaze lingered on the new pair of house slippers as Marie set the glass down on the Queen Anne nightstand and left the room. Soft and pretty, they matched the red velour robe. She traced the outline of the pale blue flowers on them. Luke hadn't just picked up anything he found. He'd taken time to choose pretty, feminine things. As if he knew deep down that these were the things she would enjoy wearing. As if he knew she'd never had these things before.

Blinking, Rachel looked around the room. The wallpaper, with its pink roses on a glimmering cream background, the satin and lace comforter on the bed, the elegant dark furniture—it all combined with her new clothes, making her more worried than ever before. The owner of the Diamond Bar seemed to have made up his mind she was staying indefinitely.

Grabbing her checkbook Rachel ran out of the room. Paying Luke for her clothes right away was the first step. She'd waited too long to assert her independence.

Luke answered the knock on his study door right away.

"Rachel, come in," he said pleasantly, when she pushed it open.

Gordie looked up and cooed in baby talk. Perched on his uncle's lap his smile reflected a cherublike innocence. Pain twisted deep inside Rachel. It was all she could do not to reach out and touch the baby.

Keeping her eyes on Luke's face she said, "Thanks for the clothes. If you'll let me know how much you spent, I'll write you a check."

The jeans and red sweater he'd picked out for her clung to her slim curves and she didn't look quite so thin. The touch of white lace at the collar drew Luke's attention to her long neck. A checkbook was clutched to her chest as if it were a shield and her stance made him smile. She reminded him of a wary doe watching a predator. One move and she would flee.

"Do they fit all right, Rae?"

Her breath snagged in her throat. Ray? The diminutive suggested a closeness she had to avoid at all costs.

"Perfectly."

Where another woman might turn around to model her new outfit she just ran the palm of her hand down her jeans.

Luke knew if he waited for her to say anything more than the absolute necessary minimum, he would wait all his life. The nickname Rae suited her perfectly. Someday soon he would tell her it meant doe in olde English and that she reminded him of one.

"Come in and see where I work."

She stepped into the bright room, her glance veering to a table by the window piled high with equipment. Luke's computer looked very sophisticated, unlike the little ones she'd seen in the old magazines shipped to MRA personnel abroad. Piles of paper rested on one end of his work area while on a smaller arm of the table, a printer was spewing out what looked like sheets of graphs.

The massive desk at the other end of the room had a leather chair behind it presently filled with Luke and baby. Luke picked up a bottle of juice and gave it to Gordie. The glow of tenderness on Luke's face as he watched Gordie drink brought a mist of tears to Rachel's eyes. Swinging away to hide them, she stared at the opposite wall.

It was covered with framed certificates. Harvard. Lucas Jasper Summers had gotten his Master's in computer science there. And another in business administration. She couldn't even remember where her high school certificate was. The wall opposite Luke held a single painting. An Indian chief on a horse.

"We used to come in here as children and sit on Grandpa Robert's knee," Luke said from behind her. "One day Rob looked at that painting and said, 'Grandpa, I want that picture.'

"'That belongs to the Diamond Bar, son,' Grandpa Robert said, 'and one day it will be yours.' It was strange." Luke burped Gordie, wiped his mouth and then set him down on the carpet. His nephew took off in a crablike crawl to a pile of toys in the corner of the room. "Even then it was Rob who wanted to run the Diamond Bar. I could ride as well as him and learned everything there was to know about raising Thoroughbreds, yet it was always math and computers for me."

"Did your parents mind?"

"No. They encouraged me as much as they did Rob. I remember them spending hours with me at math field days in local schools, even sending me to a math Camp one summer. They were as interested in working math puzzles with me as they were talking about Thoroughbreds with Rob. If they ever thought more of Rob's choice than mine, I never knew it. Even now Dad calls and the first thing he says is, 'How's your work going, son?' *Then* he talks of the ranch."

Rachel swallowed. Luke was lucky to have experienced so much love and understanding. It made it easier to understand the choices he'd made now. There was no real deliberation or sacrifice in what he'd done. Passing on what he'd received obviously came naturally.

"What made you decide on going into computer science?"

"It wasn't till I was in my last year in high school that I became acquainted with computers. I started using them for math, but then it became a game to see what else I could do with one. My parents bought me a home computer and I was hooked forever. It's a field with tremendous challenges and no limits to endeavor."

And, something told Rachel, Luke Summers was a man who needed challenges. "What did you do before the accident?"

"The company I'm with, L G and M Enterprises, develops and sells its own software. In my former position, I traveled all over the country giving one-day seminars on personal computers and spreadsheets, plus how to hone financial management skills using our software."

"And now?" He had all the right qualities for a good teacher: patience, understanding, *warmth*—plus a dynamic personality.

"Now I'm working on making changes in some of our software based on the feedback we've gotten from companies using them."

"Was it very hard to give up your former life-style and move back here?" She'd already heard Luke on this topic once before in court, but something compelled Rachel to ask him about it again.

"No," he said with conviction, his eyes swiveling to his nephew who'd thrown one toy away and was trying to bite on a huge ring. "I lived in LA because my work demanded it. I had to travel so much, it was convenient to be just a few miles away from LAX. As long as I can continue to do the work I want to, I would rather live at the Diamond Bar than anywhere in the world.''

He didn't mention how tiring constant traveling had become, how impersonal hotel rooms isolated one in a well of loneliness and how business dinners every night became more of a chore than raking out a stall.

He wanted more out of life than that now. A permanent home, a woman to share it with, Gordie, maybe some more children.

"Your lawyer said that you gave up a vice presidency to be with Gordie. Do you think that after a while that might begin to rankle?'' Rachel bit her lip. She was beginning to sound like an interviewer on a talk show.

Luke steepled his fingers and leaned back in his chair. "I put thought into a decision before I make it, weigh all the pros and cons, thrash things through in my mind. Once it's made, I never look back or indulge in what ifs.''

That he was strong she already knew. That he didn't fit the picture of men she carried in her mind, Rachel was beginning to find out. There was something else she had to say. Best get it over with quickly.

"I . . . I'm sorry I took you to court over custody of Gordie.'' Luke's head shot up. Despite the pounding of her heart Rachel held his gaze steadily. "You and the Diamond Bar are clearly what's best for him.''

"Why did you do it, Rae?''

One shoulder rose in a slight shrug. "I thought I would repay Chris for all her kindness and affection by bringing up her son.'' She raised her chin. "I also did it for myself.''

The tinge of defiance in her voice wasn't lost on Luke. From where he sat the sheen of Rachel's tears turned her irises into islands. Dark, mysterious—*enchanting*.

"For your—?'' The telephone rang, cutting him off.

"Excuse me," he reached out to pick it up, irritated by the interruption. It couldn't have come at a worse time.

Rachel heard him talking to Juan as she slipped away and went to her room. What had come over her? For a minute there she'd been about to tell him what she hadn't shared with anyone in her whole life. Rachel put a hand up to her head. The call had saved her from making a fool of herself. Luke Summers didn't need to be dumped with her personal problems. He had plenty of his own.

A frown creased her forehead. *Ray.* The way he'd shortened her name so casually had tied her up in knots. She couldn't explain the way she felt. Keyed up, excited, *alive.*

She doubted if she'd asserted anything in the study. There was a certain aura around Luke that overpowered her senses, invited her to take off her suit of armor and forget the battles she'd fought. Rachel shook her head as a red light began blinking in her brain. This visit was just a punctuation mark in her life, a temporary pause before she went back to her work. She would have to be more careful than ever not to make a fool of herself in the days that followed.

It wasn't till much later Rachel remembered she hadn't paid Luke. She would write out a blank check and ask Marie to place it on his table in the study. Going back herself would be hazardous to health.

Woken by the sunbeams flinging themselves around the room, Rachel recollected she hadn't drawn the curtains before she'd gone to sleep. She'd wanted to look out at the stars as she lay in bed. The two large windows on the opposite wall framed the sky beautifully.

Turning on her back, Rachel linked her fingers under her head and allowed her sleepy thoughts to wander.

It was forty-eight hours since the trip to Santa Barbara with Luke. Yesterday Hannah had insisted she take it easy for one more day and stay in bed. Surprisingly, a strange feeling of weakness had made her give in to the advice and rest all morning. In the afternoon, horrified by how long she'd slept, Rachel had showered and gotten as far as the family room before everyone had started fussing. She'd been put into a soft armchair, her legs wrapped in a blanket, the TV guide and remote control, a pile of magazines and a glass of freshly squeezed orange juice placed by her. Theresa sat and talked to her so she wouldn't get bored.

"There's nothing wrong with me," she'd protested to Hannah when the latter had mentioned another early night would do her good.

"Nothing that a little rest and good food won't cure," the housekeeper had agreed blandly.

Rachel had to agree all that rest had done her good. Snuggling under her comforter she closed her eyes. She felt more like her old self today.

Angela had shown her around the house yesterday when she'd come over after school. Luke's home seemed to have been designed by a master architect. It was obvious no expense had been spared in the construction of the sprawling ranch house. Yet it wasn't just a showplace. It was a home—warm, lived in, insulated with love and laughter. Generations of Summers women had seen to that.

Rachel could see Chris here clearly, talking, laughing, *loving*. Personalities she found were best described by matching them to colors. When she thought of her cousin, Rachel thought of yellow, the pale creamy yellow of a rose that spread joy just by being there. Hannah was green. Earth mother and friend. Gordie was baby blue. Innocent and lovable. Luke. Rachel's breath tangled in her throat. What color was Luke? Unbidden, purple came to mind. The rich hue of grace and royalty. A man who tempered victory with compassion.

Rachel blinked. She should have checked with Dr. Kenton about the lingering effects of jet lag. It was getting worse instead of better.

Rachel wondered what it would be like to live in one place all one's life, feel secure and loved, have a family around, watch one's babies grow into men and women and repeat the cycle of life. She could see Luke in the role of patriarch clearly. He would marry soon, have a large family. She could imagine him with graying hair, a few more lines around his eyes, looking as virile as he did now. Time wouldn't dare change the power and strength that were essentially Luke.

The tiny creak as Hannah shut her door impinged on Rachel's thoughts. Getting up, she went into the bathroom for a quick shower. Towel drying her hair, she brushed it and caught it back with an elastic band. It always dried that way. She slipped into a pair of jeans and deliberated over which sweater to wear. Her hand hovered over the red, remembering the look in Luke's eyes when he'd first seen her in it, but then she picked up the other. Emerald green and thick, it would keep her warm. Luke had chosen her clothes well. Winter mornings were cold here, though the temperature sometimes went up into the seventies in the afternoons.

"You should be taking it easy," Hannah said reprovingly as Rachel slipped into the kitchen.

"I can't possibly stay in bed any longer. Could I help you in here?" Rachel's voice trailed away. Maybe that wasn't such a good idea. From what she'd seen the kitchen was very much Hannah's domain and she might just be in the way.

"Have a cup of tea first." Hannah's smile didn't hold any resentment. "And then you can help me set the table."

Rachel sat at the table in the eating nook sipping her tea, her back toasted by the sunshine streaming in through the picture window that framed the area on one side. The large country kitchen with its blue curtains and light oak cabinets was becoming her favorite room in the house.

Sipping her tea, Rachel tried to analyze the strange feeling that she'd always been here. That she *belonged*. She shook her head and frowned. Maybe she wasn't as well as she thought she was.

"Something wrong?" Hannah was looking anxiously at her.

"No," Rachel said quickly. "I was just thinking about how much trouble I've put you all to."

"You're family," Hannah said simply. "If Chris were here, would you have felt uncomfortable about staying?"

"No," Rachel said hesitantly, "that would have been different."

"This is still Chris's home," Hannah said with irrefutable logic. "She would have wanted you to stay with us, not in some hostel in LA. Don't worry about it so, child."

Luke came in for Gordie's morning bottle, his nephew draped over his shoulder. "Good morning. Gordie and I both seemed to have overslept."

The rumpled hair and the slight stubble on Luke's chin made him look strangely vulnerable. He was wearing a maroon sweatsuit. Snug in the crook of one arm, Gordie yawned and then sucked on his fist, not fully awake yet.

Rachel looked away quickly. There was something about the picture the Summers males made together that tugged at her heartstrings, made her want to be part of it. Part of them. Her voice didn't sound quite right as she returned the greeting.

"Did you sleep well?" Luke was using his X-ray vision again on her. "Having to get used to a strange bed didn't keep you up did it?"

"No . . . I slept very well."

Rachel rose and rinsed her cup, loading it into the dishwasher. She was taking out the table mats when she sensed him leave with Gordie. He seemed to take some of her tension with him. Rachel let out a long breath and looked up to see Hannah watching her.

"The house is so beautiful." It was the only thing she could think of to say. The oddly speculative look on Hannah's face made her nervous.

"The original farmhouse was much smaller." The housekeeper turned away to the counter and started getting breakfast. "When Grandpa Robert gave them his blessing Miriam and Gordon knew things would be very hard at first."

"Go on," Rachel prompted, watching Hannah pour flour into a bowl, measure it with a glance and add some buttermilk. The urge to know more about the history of the Summers family was inexplicable but very strong.

"They mortgaged everything to buy a two-year-old colt, Jupiter's Gold, the year Rob was born. That was when I came to work for them. Miriam spent every waking hour with that horse, training him, loving him. Buying him was a gamble. His sire had good lines but hadn't achieved anything spectacular in the racing world, his mother had never raced. Jupiter wasn't the best, just the best they could afford, but hard work and love paid off. He won the Triple Crown that year to everyone's amazement. With his winnings Miriam and Gordon bought three more yearlings to train and race. Miriam was great with horses but Gordon's business brain had a great deal to do with their success, as well. They had Luke eighteen months after Rob and hired a girl to help me in the house so I could devote all my time to the boys. Luke was three when they decided to build here instead of renovating the old farmhouse.

Biscuits in the oven, Hannah poured oat bran into boiling water and stirred it briskly as she continued, "The Diamond Bar quickly developed a reputation for training winners. Jupiter's Gold was our first stud stallion. The boys were three and five when their parents decided to stop training and concentrate totally on breeding Thoroughbreds. The children were growing so quickly and the racing circuit was taking too much out of their family life. Miriam found she couldn't have any more children and that had a great deal to do with the decision, as well. They wanted to enjoy the two they had."

Hannah placed the bowl of steaming oat bran on the table, along with fresh fruit, biscuits and butter, and stood back and looked at everything as Luke returned with his beaming nephew. Rachel's heart twisted at the sight of the freshly bathed and powdered baby. The fine hair brushed to one side gave him a pin neat look that wouldn't last five minutes. With his cheeks glowing and baby teeth showing in an affable grin, Chris's son looked the picture of health and contentment.

Placing Gordie on his exercise mat, Luke sat down at the table and helped himself to the hot cereal.

"Do you ride, Rachel?"

"I only rode on the farm with Chris, years ago." Placid horses that understood nervous riders.

"It's like riding a bike . . . one doesn't forget how." Luke reached for the milk. "We have some nice quiet horses we keep just for riding. Pick one out at the stables today and call the farm office whenever you feel like riding and Juan will dispatch one of the grooms to the house. There's just one rule though."

"Rule?" Rachel had no intention of riding, but the word piqued her interest. These last few days had taught her one thing. Luke didn't lay down the law. He stated it and everyone else followed his example of keeping it. For him to do so now there had to be a special reason.

"You don't ride alone, ever."

She didn't miss the quick intent look Hannah gave Luke before turning away.

Rachel ate her cereal thoughtfully. Was Luke afraid she would get lost and cause more trouble than she already had? It didn't seem worthwhile to remind them she wouldn't be here long enough to do that. She didn't want to hone her riding skills, because where she was going she wouldn't need them.

Rachel bit into a biscuit, surprised by the anger that shook her. It had been a while since she'd felt this deeply about anything. Convincing Luke she wasn't a permanent fixture at the Diamond Bar assumed paramount importance all of a sudden, but she couldn't argue in front of Hannah. She would talk to him later.

Each day he found yet another thing to bind her to this place. Gordie, unlimited hospitality, a horse of her own. True, they were silken chains but nonetheless alarming. If he kept this up she would never be able to leave.

Rachel sighed. What did it take to get through to the man? He acted as if she had no other life, as if she were home where she belonged.

"Are you going to show Rachel around the farm this morning?" Hannah asked.

"Might as well." Reaching for an apple, Luke bit into it. "Then she'll feel more at home."

More at home? Rachel wanted to say something brilliant and explicit, but the words tangled with the emotion in her throat and stuck there.

"If you can be ready I'd like to leave in half an hour." There was nothing in his expression to indicate showing her around was anything more than common courtesy. Maybe her imagination still hadn't gotten over the jet lag. Rachel murmured concurrence, and rose to help Hannah clear the table.

It took ten minutes in the pickup following a road that wrapped the mountainside to get to the farm. Surprised when he pulled up two hundred yards from the gate, Rachel turned to Luke.

"Look."

She followed the gesture of his head and blinked. Slightly below them was a huge valley. Lush and green, it nestled at the foothills like a jewel in a crown. Mountains rose like giant sentinels all around it. Rachel stared at the scene in silence. It was like going through a magic door into a different world. The beehive of activity reminded her of a county fair. There were people and horses everywhere. Large wide buildings dominated the northeastern portion. In the middle of all the big structures sat a small red building that looked like a house. The rest of the land was taken up by huge paddocks with horses in them. Scents and sounds combined to print her first look at the farm indelibly on her mind. This was bigger than anything she'd ever imagined.

"Welcome to the Diamond Bar, Rae." She sensed Luke's watchful air and wasn't sure what kind of a reaction was expected of her.

"It's hard to believe all this is just around the corner from the house," she said.

The sight in front of her rendered her unable to say more. From Chris's letters she'd derived a picture of a small farm, with a few horses. Even from this distance she could see that the Diamond Bar was a large-scale business operation.

"Mom and Dad planned it like this." Luke put the truck in gear and they moved forward. "They wanted their private life to be just that—private. They loved their work but they didn't want it to dominate their living space. This valley is perfect for the horses."

Waving to a man by the gate, Luke pulled up directly in front of the red building. The word office was painted in six-inch high, white letters.

A man passed them, raising a hand in casual salute. The gorgeous animal with him had a black coat that looked like liquid coal. Rachel took a step back as the horse went by, feeling intimidated by its size. She watched as it was led into what was obviously a large stable. Looking around, she noticed there were six large buildings, each with a number clearly marked on it.

Luke gestured toward the cottages nestling in the mountainside and a long building that reminded her of army barracks she'd seen once. "Staff quarters. We have a little community of our own here, even a small store."

Rachel wet her lips. The feeling that she was on the set of a movie intensified. Maybe she was in the middle of one of those dreams that left her soaked with sweat and terrified to go back to sleep. She hadn't had one for a long time now. Looking at Luke, she tried to smile.

"We have stud stallions here that are syndicated for over twenty million dollars each." Luke made his voice as matter-of-fact as possible. The look in her eyes made him uneasy. Maybe he should have given her a hint of all this earlier. "Each yearling foal costs anywhere between half a million and a million dollars."

"Is security a problem?" A vague memory of a television show where a horse's markings had been changed and the animal smuggled out of the country, surfaced.

"The whole area is under video camera surveillance, as well as being patrolled by our own security men. Tom, the man at the gate, knows everyone who works here." He didn't tell her the two men working in the grounds around the house were there for security reasons, as well. Or that the rule of not riding alone was to ensure her safety. Or that telephoned threats were part of the business.

"What is a syndicated stallion?"

She knew so little about Thoroughbreds. The fact that breeding them was a multimillion dollar enterprise was just beginning to sink in. And to think she'd wanted Gordie— had thought she would be able to provide for all his needs. . . .

"We buy stallions with good racing records and shares are sold in each one's breeding career," Luke explained. "Each shareholder has the opportunity of breeding one mare to the stallion he has a share in, every year. If a shareholder doesn't have a mare, he's paid half a million dollars, which is the approximate cost of one breeding for anyone who isn't a shareholder these days."

"I see." She didn't. Not really. But she had the main picture. Money, money and more money.

Luke was a rich man in his own right. *Very* rich. The fact that he still worked at a regular job was by choice not necessity. What on earth had his reaction been when he'd heard she was taking him to court over custody of Gordie?

Theresa had mentioned something yesterday about it being wonderful the way things had turned out. Gordie was where he belonged and she was part of the family, as well. Apparently they had all been worried for a while there.

Rachel's fists seemed to clench of their own accord. Did everyone here know about her pathetic attempt to gain custody of Gordon Summers?

She must have outdone the Lucy show for laughs per minute.

# Chapter Five

They were at the door of the first stable. Rachel followed Luke into it. Any novice could tell no money had been spared here, either. The spotlessly clean place was a fitting environment for the majestic horses full of restless energy.

"Stable A is where we keep our stud stallions," Luke said as he stopped by a stall to pat one animal's broad forehead. Rachel kept well back. She wasn't sure how these horses would react to strangers and she wasn't about to risk finding out. "They each have their own paddocks, as well."

"Their own paddocks?"

"Yes, that's the best way for stallions. Very rarely do we put two stallions together. They might fight and injure each other. Sometimes a stallion has a mare or two with him in his paddock but most of them are alone. In addition to running on their own they're ridden regularly to keep them in top condition."

Rachel stared at the bay that was rolling its eyes at her, glad she didn't have the job of riding one of these huge creatures.

"The few that are inside are either waiting for the vet or are being kept in because they're not well," Luke explained, continuing to caress the bay's broad forehead. "We don't take any chances with them."

Not when they were worth a few million apiece, Rachel agreed silently.

At a rough estimate the stable contained twenty stalls. Multiply that by twenty million and... Rachel's head began to spin. Whoever kept count of all that money must have to work overtime.

The horses themselves were magnificent. She could understand how anyone would find them fascinating. The ripple of powerful muscles under shiny coats, the majestic arch of the neck, the regal bearing, put them in a class of their own. Every movement was like poetry in motion.

A tiny sound at odds with the pawing of hooves, the snorts and neighs caught Rachel's attention. Tilting her head she listened.

Luke turned to her in surprise as she clutched his sleeve. "Am I hearing things or is there a goat in here?"

Luke nodded, the half smile on his face making her hot despite the cool December morning. She tried to snatch her hand back but he held it tightly, as if it were the most natural thing in the world as they walked to another stall farther down. There, tied next to the largest stallion Rachel had seen so far, was a tiny black-and-white goat. Unperturbed by its surroundings, or the creature twenty times its weight moving around beside it, the goat nibbled at the hay in the hay net.

Rachel's eyes rounded in wonder. "Meet Rainbow's End," Luke said casually. "He retired as a four-year-old after winning two and a half million dollars on the race-track. When Rob brought him home he just wouldn't settle. He kept throwing himself around and we were afraid he'd hurt himself. His last owner was out of the country and we couldn't get through to his trainer. Finally Mom suggested bringing Nellie in from the fields. The change in Rainbow's End was dramatic. He'll do anything as long as Nellie stays with him.''

Rachel stared at the odd couple. It was strange to think an animal as strong and magnificent as this Thoroughbred in front of them could be so utterly dependent on the tiny goat for its happiness. It reminded her of the parable of the lion and the mouse; of strength that had nothing to do with size or muscle; of needing and being needed.

A groom came looking for Luke with a message from Juan. A Mr. Callaghan from Ireland wanted to talk to him.

"I won't be long," he told Rachel and she wondered if she'd imagined the note of resignation in his voice.

Wandering out to the nearest paddock, Rachel leaned against the white fence enjoying the sun on her back, the breeze in her face. There were about six yearlings within the fence's confines, their actions reminding her of children at play.

"Good morning."

She turned and smiled at Jason Harrington, the farm accountant. He'd come up to the house yesterday afternoon with Juan Rodriguez to meet her. Jason and Luke had gone to school together. Now, Rachel wondered if the visit had been to check her out. Evidently she'd passed muster because the smile accompanying the greeting held no reservations.

"Good morning," Rachel returned.

"Seeing how we work?"

"Yes. Luke's showing me around, but he got a telephone call and had to go in for a bit."

"Lucky for me." Jason's smile widened. "Want to take a closer look at the yearlings?"

They were halfway to the second paddock when a man passed them carrying a coil of rope and some other equipment.

"Mojo's a handler," Jason explained. "He's going to spend some time with Gulliver, our favorite two-year-old colt."

Though dressed like the other men, the handler's shoulder-length hair and pronounced features told Rachel he was at least part Indian.

"How's the leg, Mojo?" Jason asked in passing.

"Not too good, Jason, not too good."

Rachel couldn't help noticing the pronounced limp the man walked with.

"What's wrong with his leg?" Rachel asked as soon as they were was out of earshot.

"I don't know." Jason shrugged, his eyes on the colt Mojo was signaling to. "He's been favoring it for days now. Won't let a doctor look at it. Says he's treating it himself but it seems to be getting worse."

"I thought the foals were sold as yearlings?"

Rachel's brow creased in a slight frown as she looked at the colt being fitted with a halter. It looked much bigger than the ones in the next paddock.

"Gulliver's the exception. He broke his leg last year just before the January sales and Rob wanted to make sure it healed properly. If he'd been pushed into training too early it might have resulted in another break, so Rob refused to sell him. Mojo cared for him and when he was completely healed he began to give him some basic training."

"Will he be sold this year?"

The colt was snuffling the man's shoulder, its actions showing more clearly than any words the rapport between them.

"I guess so. We aren't a training farm any longer and that colt is the result of some mighty fine breeding."

Mojo began putting a halter on the horse. Rachel watched as he tried to get the horse to stand still. His face had a sallow tinge that seemed at odds with the color of his skin. A grimace of pain squeezed his features as he stepped back.

"That's the position they need in halter class," Jason explained, "the younger they learn the easier it is for them later when they're sold and their regular training begins. Mojo's trying to get Gulliver to stand on all four feet square and hold his neck and tail high."

It required a great deal of patience. As Jason watched the colt, Rachel looked at Mojo's face. The sweat beaded on the man's forehead told her all she needed to know.

"He's in pain," she said quietly. "He has to see a doctor."

Jason looked surprised. "I told you, he won't go."

"Will he let me look at it?"

Jason's jaw dropped. Rachel didn't wait for an answer. She was on familiar ground now. Whirling, she went over to Mojo. Face-to-face he didn't look as old as she'd thought him to be . . . he was barely into his twenties and behind the resentment in his gaze she glimpsed uncertainty.

"What's wrong with your leg?"

As the startled colt took off, annoyance was clearly visible on Mojo's face, but Rachel didn't budge.

"Nothing," he muttered. "It's just a boil."

"Where?"

For a minute it looked as if he wasn't going to answer her question. Jason cleared his throat and with a shrug the man pointed to his thigh. Rachel's eyes widened as she took in the damp stain on his jeans. Inky red, it confirmed what she'd suspected.

"It's not just a boil. It looks like an abscess that's ruptured. The infection in your system is what's causing the pain. You'll have to have it lanced and drained and go on a course of antibiotics. I wouldn't be surprised if you have a fever, as well."

She leaned forward and put her hand on the man's forehead ignoring his start of surprise. "You're burning up!"

"It's nothing," he said angrily.

"You know what can happen to it if you don't get it treated?" She could have been discussing the weather with a friend, her tone was so ordinary. "Your leg will get so bad gangrene might set in. Is your foolish pride going to make up for the loss of your leg when ten minutes with a doctor will take care of everything?"

Checkmate. No one moved or spoke for a few minutes. Jason swallowed nervously. Luke had sent him out here to keep Rachel company, not start a field clinic. He only hoped his report would sound as convincing as her tone.

"I've seen many men like you," Rachel said softly. "Cowards. Big and strong, but afraid of being sick, of the very medicine that can heal them."

She'd touched a raw nerve all right. Mojo looked absolutely livid. He clenched his hands into fists as he gritted out, "I'm not afraid."

"I'm so glad to hear that. You have to see a doctor right away." She turned to Jason. "Can someone take him down to have his leg attended to? I can change the dressing for him tomorrow."

The Indian turned and stomped off without a word. Jason followed, his eyebrows threatening to disappear into his hairline. He was back in a few minutes.

"It wasn't just fear motivating him to keep on working," Rachel said thoughtfully. "What was the other reason, do you know?"

"Well," Jason pushed the Stetson he was never without to the back of his head and said, "it could be that he's on daily wages and if he doesn't work, he doesn't get paid. Besides, the men on the regular payroll have medical benefits, but the daily workers don't."

"That's not fair." The look she shot him boded ill for stupid rules. "Anyone can see he's really ill. Exceptions have to be made in cases like this."

"Cases like what?"

Neither of them had heard Luke come up behind them. Rachel explained about Mojo, finishing with, "Can't you bend the rules for a case like Mojo's, Luke? Anyone can see the man's in dire need of medical attention. Jason says if you insist he rest for a day he'll just go somewhere else and work. It's not fair, either, that someone on minimum wage should have to pay his own medical bill."

She'd turned into a tigress over a stranger's cause? Luke looked at her flashing eyes and heaving chest and wondered if it would always take someone else's needs to make Rae ready to take on the world. Would she ever learn to ask for what she herself needed out of life?

"Call Dr. Kenton and tell him to bill the Diamond Bar for Mojo's treatment," he told Jason. "Then tell Mojo he can have sick time off with pay. If any of the other men grumble, tell them the change applies to them as well as long as they can produce a certificate from a doctor. Let Juan know what I've just told you."

"Thank you." Rachel looked away from Luke at the yearlings, not wanting him to see the wealth of emotion in her eyes. She wasn't sure it was only gratitude he would find there.

He wondered what she would have done if he'd refused to change things. Probably pay for Mojo's treatment herself. Luke had never met anyone who cared less about money. The blank check he'd found on his study table attested to that.

Behind the house a trail wound through the trees and led to a grove of evergreens arranged in a perfect circle. Rachel sank onto the fallen tree trunk that served as a seat and rested against the trunk of another. This had to be the most beautiful spot in the world. She had a panoramic view. On the horizon she could see the Pacific. Below her lay the house, hidden from view by a row of Italian cypress.

Today, however, her mind wasn't on the view. It was time to reconsider her position.

She'd been at the Diamond Bar an entire week now and each day it seemed like one of the bricks in her carefully constructed defense crumbled. She was closer to being more seriously hurt than she'd ever been in her life. It was time to take a dispassionate look at what was happening and stop it before it got out of hand.

What was happening was that she was dangerously close to forgetting every harsh lesson she'd ever learned—of letting herself get accustomed to things, of believing again.

That wasn't all. For someone who untill very recently had worked twenty-hour days she was getting so used to Hannah's cosseting, and life in the lap of luxury, it was going to be difficult to get back to normal.

Luke. Rachel bent forward, picked up a spray of pine needles and twirled it between her thumb and forefinger. He treated her as if she were Gordie's age. Didn't argue. Didn't plead. Just listened and then went ahead and did exactly as he wanted. Rachel knew something now that she'd never experienced in her whole life. Strong men used the word "yes" to get their own way.

Hannah. Rachel wanted to throw her arms around the older woman and hug her for all the warmth and love she exuded. To someone who had this deep void inside, as Rachel did, just being around the housekeeper was enough to dispel any emptiness.

Theresa Rodriguez had taken her visiting one afternoon and introduced her to the other wives on the Diamond Bar. She was welcomed as Chris's cousin, asked about her work abroad, urged to come back and visit. Rachel had come away with the feeling that these people liked her for who she was.

Jason had offered to teach her how to ride, how to drive and how to square dance. He made her laugh with his jokes and his easygoing comments on life. Every Friday night, he'd told her, the farm employees had a get-together in the old barn that had been converted to a huge recreation area. Any time she felt like joining them he would be happy to escort her. Rachel thanked him politely but refused all the offers. She wasn't going to be there long enough to benefit from any of the lessons.

In the ranch house, Luke and Hannah seemed to have entered into a conspiracy. She wasn't allowed to help around the house. When they weren't urging her to eat, they were shooing her outdoors, telling her to get some fresh air into her lungs. Neither of them asked why she hadn't picked up the baby yet. Neither of them seemed to mind.

For the first time in her personal life, other than the brief summer she'd spent with Christina, Rachel found herself being accepted for who she was, no strings attached. The feeling was heady and dangerous.

A person could get addicted to that kind of thing, delude oneself that it would last. The fact remained that she didn't belong here, and the sooner she got back to her normal routine the better.

She'd talked to Dr. Waylon Smith, Director of the MRA chapter in LA yesterday. He'd already received two telephone calls about her. That had been another surprise. One, call he said, had been from a Luke Summers, the other from a Dr. Kenton in Santa Barbara. She wasn't to think of returning until Dr. Kenton gave her a clean bill of health. The New Year would be time enough to talk about her next assignment. If she wanted, there was a position in LA she could have, interviewing and training volunteers for relief work abroad.

It had taken that telephone call to make Rachel realize how determined Luke was to keep her at the Diamond Bar. That he cared for what was his, she could see every day she spent here. What frightened her was that for some reason, he was beginning to include her in that category. Had he suggested to Dr. Smith that she should be offered a local job?

The thought was tempting. If she lived in LA she could see Gordon often. Luke, she knew, would be generous about allowing her to visit.

A crow cawed, interrupting her wishful thinking. That was all it amounted to. Toying with the idea of staying here was just opening the way to more rejection. Any fool could see the way she was reacting to Luke already was out of all proportion to the impersonal, kind hospitality she was being offered. How long would she be content with that? Given time she would want more, and that was when the trouble would begin.

Christmas was three weeks away. She had to get away before that.

* * *

Hannah glared at Luke. "Did Dr. Kenton tell you what's

wrong with her? She hasn't held the baby yet. Watches him with her heart in her eyes when no one's around. I've never seen anything like it in all my seventy years.''

"Give her time." Luke sounded angry.

Hannah knew he wasn't angry with her. Or Rachel. He was just angry with whatever had made her the way she was. It had to have been a bitter lesson to make Rachel Carstairs afraid of loving.

"Maybe we ought to force the issue a bit." Luke's brow furrowed in thought. "Get you out of the way."

"You mean say I'm sick and send Marie home early?"

Luke nodded. "Your bad back could give out on you, or you could fall and break a bone in your ankle." Warming to his idea he continued thoughtfully, "Just something to put her in the position where she *has* to pick up Gordie."

Hannah swiped him with the kitchen towel she always kept on her shoulder. "Get back to your work, you wily old fox, before I find that old wooden spoon I used on you and Rob. You'll have me in a straitjacket next."

But the idea took root. Rachel returned from her walk to find Hannah moaning, seated in a straight-backed chair, obviously in pain. Gordie sat nearby, listening to the sounds with interest, trying to make similar sounds of his own.

"Hannah, what's wrong?" Rachel was on her knees beside the chair in a second.

"My back," Hannah groaned, "I just reached forward in a certain way and it went click. Ooh!"

"I'll call Dr. Kenton." Rachel's initial concern was ousted by a professional calm that had stood her in good stead for the past four and a half years.

"Luke already did that." Hannah sounded breathless and Rachel wondered if she was more shaken than she was letting on. "This has happened before. Dr. Kenton said I was

to alternate hot and cold treatments, take my muscle relax-
ant and painkillers and sleep on a firm mattress."

Luke stepped into the kitchen. "Hannah, are you any
better?"

Hannah bit her lip and shook her head. "Jason was going
into town and I gave Marie the afternoon off so she could
get some early Christmas shopping done."

"Well, don't worry about that now. Let's get you to bed
first." His brow creased in a frown. "Juan just called.
Theresa can't come in today, either. David's running a fever. Angela will be over as soon as she's home from school,
but that won't be for awhile. Pity Marie picked today to go
shopping. I have to finish this new program I'm working on
by tomorrow. I won't be able to do that now. I'll just call my
office and—"

"Don't do that, Luke," Rachel interrupted quickly, "I
can help."

The metamorphosis to calm, capable, confident woman
amazed Luke. Any hint of shyness, uncertainty, was gone.
Aware Rae was talking he forced himself to concentrate.
"Let me help Hannah to bed and I'll be right back. I have a
general idea of Gordie's routine, and I can manage to keep
him busy when he's awake. It'll work out." Turning to
Hannah she said soothingly, "It will wear off in a day or
two, you'll see."

Cued by Luke's raised brows, Hannah wheezed in mock
sorrow, "No, it won't. It's been like this before. Always
takes at least a week to mend."

An arm around her, Rachel helped Hannah to her room.
She returned after a while and said brusquely, "I'll keep an
eye on Gordie now."

Luke held out a piece of paper with Gordie's schedule on
it. "His formula's already made up in the refrigerator. Baby

food's on the shelf above the toaster. If you need any help, just yell."

His eyes held hers, searching the depths for signs of nervousness and finding none. Rachel Carstairs must be one hell of a good relief worker. Not many women could match her response in a crisis. He shrugged slightly. "I guess I'd better get back to the computer."

It was as simple as that.

Two hours later Luke peeped into the sun room. Only the movement of the rocker gave any indication Rachel was in it. Singing. The melody of a lullaby floated to him. Luke looked up at the glass of the patio door. Her reflection showed her cheek resting on Gordie's head. The baby was fast asleep, but it was easy to see she wasn't going to put him down for a while.

Luke smiled, though the lump in his throat was painful. Maybe Gordie would get the message across to Rachel that she belonged here. He slipped away to check on Hannah.

"It's working," he announced triumphantly. "Heard her talking to Gordie all the time she was giving him his lunch. Heard her laugh out loud once, and now she's singing to him."

Pleasure flooded Hannah. She hadn't seen Luke look so relaxed in a long while. Not wanting to embarrass either of them, she covered emotion with gruffness. "How long do I have to stay in here? Lying in bed is a penance. Rachel took my pillows away. Said it was better for my back this way. I can barely breathe in this position."

"Rest easy. It won't be for more than a week, I promise."

Luke's careless whistle could be heard all the way back to his study. A week! Hannah glared at the door he'd closed behind him. Inaction would be the death of her.

She wasn't really angry, though. Getting her pillows out of the closet she propped herself up and leaned back with a satisfied smile on her face.

"It does a body good to hear him whistle," she said aloud.

Miriam Summers had been excellent with the Thoroughbreds, sharing all the duties of running the Diamond Bar with her husband. It had been Hannah who'd brought up the boys those first few years, forging a bond with them that had never slackened. Now, one of her boys was dead. She wanted happiness for the other, not a lifetime of abasement of his own needs so he could do the right thing by his brother's son. Sometimes Luke's total involvement with Gordie frightened her.

"My sister Betty wants me to visit her," Hannah announced when Rachel carried a tray in at one o'clock. She'd barely managed to push the pillows off the bed in time. "Did I tell you she lives just half an hour away? Well, I talked to her and she said she'd love some company. It would make it easier for you, too, not having to wait on me hand and foot."

"I don't mind the work," Rachel protested. The rope tied to the anchor was slipping through Rachel's hands fast and she made one last desperate grab at it. "Hannah, don't—"

"Yes, dear?" Hannah peered at the soup, ignoring the panic in the face above hers. Not waiting for an answer she swept on. "It will be good to visit with Betty. Did I tell you her husband, Bud, is away in San Francisco for the week? A business trip, but this close to Christmas she couldn't go with him. She's inundated with orders for her baked goods. Betty and I have always been very close. She's so excited about my visit, I feel better already."

It would be selfish to say anything. Rachel bit her lip. She would miss the warm, garrulous housekeeper terribly.

"It's all arranged." Hannah nodded her head in satisfaction, pretending she couldn't see the look of desperation on Rachel's face. "Luke knows how to make up Gordie's formula. He's managed on his own before. Theresa has offered to come in from eight to one with Marie. Angela usually gets here about three and stays till six. She'll return at eight and sleep here all the time I'm away. You'll do just fine. Gordie very seldom gets up at night, so you don't have to worry about that. Luke has the baby monitor in his room anyway, and he's in Gordie's room before the child can draw breath for his second cry. Juan will drop me off at my sister's ... save her making the trip. Remember I'm only a phone call away."

Rachel packed a bag for Hannah. Half an hour later the housekeeper had left and the house seemed very empty. For someone with a bad back, she was surprisingly agile getting into the car, Rachel noticed. Backs were tricky things. Hopefully, Hannah wouldn't suffer too much pain with hers.

There was no sign of Luke since an hour ago when he'd fixed them both roast beef sandwiches for lunch, and asked if she needed any help.

Gordie was still asleep. Rachel sank into the rocker in the family room and took a deep breath. She would manage fine...as long as she didn't panic. And she wouldn't frighten herself by trying to look at the picture of the whole week stretching ahead. Just the next hour. That was the way she'd gotten through some of the worst situations in her relief work.

Angela's arrival coincided with Gordie waking up. The girl had a well-established routine. She plugged in the vacuum cleaner and got busy.

Gordie needed changing. Rachel carried him to his room, deciding to sponge his face and change his clothes, as well.

The first part was no problem. He smiled as she wielded the washcloth wrung out in warm water. Putting him into a diaper was a different matter altogether. The children she'd worked with had rarely used diapers. The few she'd seen had been cloth ones that fastened with a knot in front, or a safety pin. Tongue between her teeth, Rachel managed to get it on him. She thought she'd done pretty well till she picked him up and it slid off his little bottom. Luckily the tapes were resealable. Rachel tried again. How tight was too tight for a baby?

Pleased with her second attempt, she finished dressing Gordie and took him into the family room. It was all a matter of staying calm and getting used to doing things differently, she told herself. Taking out a bottle, she plugged in the bottle warmer. Gordie nestled into her neck. Pleasure so intense it was almost painful shot through Rachel, and she laughed softly, "You're a sweetheart. I'm falling in love with you."

"Another slave?"

Rachel's heart jerked, then went completely still. Luke stood in the doorway watching them. Time froze for a minute and she had the oddest feeling they were replaying a familiar scene from another time, another life.

"Need a hand?" He was so close she couldn't think, couldn't breathe. The warmth that emanated from him invited touching. The crisp curls in the vee of his checked shirt were oddly disturbing.

"No. He's fine." Rachel turned away, picked up the bottle. Gordie in his usual rush grabbed at it. The smile returned to Rachel's face as she sank onto the wooden rocker, cradling him in her arms. Gordie seemed to think feeding time was an aerobic workout. If she kept her mind on the baby, the rest would just fade away.

Luke strolled over to a kitchen cabinet, took out a couple of mugs and placed the kettle on the stove.

"Want some herbal tea?"

A week here and the craving for coffee had disappeared. "Please. How's the job going?"

Luke's eyes lingered on the baby's dark head tucked into the curve of Rachel's breast. "Fine. I should be done by midnight. Tomorrow I can give you a hand with Gordie."

He poured the boiling water over the tea bags. For the first time, Rachel noticed the lines of strain around his eyes. "Don't worry about us. We're getting along fine."

"I can see that."

Gordie's eyes were fixed on Rachel's face as he drank. Rachel looked down at him, and the indescribable tenderness she felt cast a startling luminescence on her features. Luke drank in the picture. The sight was enough to bring a strong man to his knees in reverence. He fought the urge to pick them both up and hold them close to his heart.

It was too soon. Rachel was walking a tightrope of discovery. About herself. About life. One wrong move on his part and she would tumble off and never find the courage to get back on. He had to be patient. It was a first for him, this waiting for a woman, but then he wanted more than a brief roll in the hay with Rachel.

"Leave mine on the counter, please."

Her voice jerked him back to the present. Nodding, he picked up his own mug and went back to the study.

On the family room floor, Rachel played a game of peek-a-boo with Gordie that set him giggling and chuckling. After a while she put him on his exercise mat, reminding herself that he could roll over and crawl. Yesterday Hannah said he'd gotten behind the couch in the family room and almost given her a heart attack when she'd looked up and hadn't seen him anywhere. Luckily, he'd cooed an immediate answer to her call.

Dinner. Thinking of the wonderful meals Hannah always had on the table, Rachel was consumed by nervousness. When it had been just her father and herself, the evening meal had usually been canned soup and sandwiches. Once in a while she'd put things into a Crockpot, but that was the extent of her culinary talents. There had never been any opportunity to learn to cook abroad. MRA usually hired a local cook for the field-workers. Surely it couldn't be too difficult. Hannah made it look so easy.

An hour later she wasn't so sure. Gordie was bored. He let her know by whining. The kitchen was a shambles. Rachel felt as if she'd just been through an aerobic workout herself without enjoying any of the benefits. In the oven she had a couple of pork chops, which if they cooperated, would be dinner. Leftover potato salad would accompany it. She stared at the cluttered counters around her. Such a big mess for one meal.

Gordie began to cry in earnest. Temporarily abandoning the thought of cleaning the kitchen, Rachel picked him up and hugged him. He was soaked through.

"Oh, dear!" Evidently her diapering skills were on the same level as her culinary skills.

Gordie seemed to agree. He started yelling his little head off.

Suddenly Luke was there, relieving her of the angry baby. He pulled his arm out from under Gordie and looked a little startled at the wet patch on his sleeve, but all he said was, "I'll fix him up in a jiffy. Why don't you put your feet up for a little while?"

He was gone before she could protest that she would change Gordie. Not that she wanted to. Those diapers seemed to sense she couldn't fasten them right. Life seemed very difficult all of a sudden. Rachel's chin wobbled as a sense of failure flooded her.

An acrid smell had her rushing to the oven. Grabbing a mitt but not bothering to slip her hand into it, she pulled out the tray.

"Ouch!" She'd gotten too close to the heating element at the top of the oven. Thumping the tray down on the counter, she rushed over to the tap and ran cold water over her hand. Behind her, two blackened blobs rested in a pan that would need a month of scouring to get it back to Hannah's standard of clean. She must have set the oven too high. Her hand smarted and two tears escaped and rolled down her face. Tossing the chops into the garbage, Rachel replaced the tray and slammed the oven door shut. Could one make sandwiches with potato salad?

Luke reentered the kitchen in a clean shirt, with a fresh-smelling baby who was all smiles again. Tactfully, he ignored the smoke and her flushed face as he took out two jars of baby food and placed them in the microwave.

"I've burned the dinner." The belligerent tone reminded him of a cornered Chihuahua.

"There's pizza in the freezer," Luke returned quietly. "I'll heat it up as soon as Gordie finishes eating."

Ignoring the chaos around him, he began to feed Gordie ham and peas. It wasn't till he heard the door of Rachel's room shut behind her did he allow himself a sweeping glance of the kitchen.

A half smile on his lips he said to Gordie, "Better not get her a cookbook for Christmas, champ."

## Chapter Six

After Gordie was settled for the night, Luke lit a fire in the family room fireplace. There was no sign of Rachel. He wondered if she'd opted for one of her long baths. It was her one pastime that amused everyone. After dinner one evening, Hannah had asked her if she would like to watch a popular nighttime soap with her. Rachel had hesitated and then said, "If you don't mind, I'd rather take a bath."

He'd thrown her into the deep end today. She'd surprised him again with her ability to cope, her quiet maturity... and impressed him. He knew very few women who could step in and take over a job like this without any notice at all, without making a song and dance about it.

There had been quite a few rough spots. His gut tightened as he thought of her woebegone expression when he'd pulled his sleeve out from under a soaking wet Gordie. And that dinner. He hadn't thought she would attempt to cook anything. Hannah always kept the freezer stocked with precooked meals, and he really should have said something about it.

Luke looked up to see the object of his thoughts standing in the doorway dressed in a multicolored wraparound skirt and a soft white blouse with a scooped neckline that exposed the vulnerable hollows at the base of her throat. Her hair was pulled back in a knot, the damp tendrils that nestled against her neck lingering evidence of a shower. The stamp of uncertainty was back on her face . . . as if without Gordie or Hannah there to hide behind, she was lost.

Luke's mouth tightened again. How long was it going to take to earn her trust?

"Would you like something to drink, Rae?"

Her eyes flickered as she looked at the glass of amber fluid in his hand. "No . . . no thank you."

"Come, sit down. The pizza will be ready in five minutes. I called Hannah and she's doing fine."

"I'm glad." Rachel advanced into the room, sat down on an armchair, picked up a cushion and hugged it to her slight frame. "How old is Hannah?"

"Seventy."

"She looks about fifty and has so much energy. She makes everything look so easy." The wistfulness wasn't lost on Luke.

"You did just great today."

The crimson tide that stole up her face amazed him. Surely, he thought, she knows how good she is. If the way she'd stepped in and handled everything was any indication of how she worked, *someone* had to have told Rachel Carstairs she was worth her weight in gold.

He watched as she twisted her fingers together and then said deliberately, "You're so good with Gordie. I'm amazed at the way he's taken to you. He's beginning to recognize people and fusses with strangers after a few minutes, but everytime I looked in on the two of you, you were getting on famously. I never expected to get so much work done today. Thank you, Rae."

She lifted her head quickly and he caught the reflection of the fire in the sheen of her tears. Leaning forward, Luke reached for her. He couldn't deny himself the comfort he wanted to offer her any longer.

The timer went off in the kitchen and she jumped up. "I'll set the table."

Watching her scurry away, he could tell the charged atmosphere between them made her very uneasy.

"Let's eat in here. It's nicer by the fire," Luke called after her.

Rachel paused and looked back over one shoulder. It *was* nicer by the fire. Too nice.

Her heart's usually even rhythm had changed to a staccato beat. Luke looked different tonight. His stone-washed jeans and soft blue shirt seemed molded to his frame. Seated on the floor, long legs stretched out in front of him, he looked absolutely relaxed. The fire glinted off his face, etching the strong lines in gold. His eyes sparkled with intent, the look in them both frightening and exciting her.

It had to be the fire that instilled so much excitement in the atmosphere, cloaking the normally cheery room with enchantment and mystery. The orange flames cast exotic patterns on the weathered gray stone and the whole room looked different in its glow.

Did he know she'd never been in a situation like this before? That every moment seemed tinged with magic? Swallowing hard, Rachel carried the plates to the coffee table and prepared to go back for the rest.

Luke's hand on her shoulder made her jump. His command was as strong as it was soft. "Sit. Relax. I'll get the rest."

She'd been touched before. Often. But even the briefest of contact with this man produced the electricity that left her witless. Rachel sank onto a cushion, refusing to look up when he returned with the glasses, set them down and went back for the pizza.

Sitting down across from her, Luke picked up the piece of pizza she served him and bit into it, ignoring the cutlery. "It's good." The obvious satisfaction in his tone after the first bite drew no visible response from her.

Rachel pretended to be absorbed by the fire, while every nerve ending in her body danced in awareness of Luke. He reached for the hot peppers and his arm brushed against hers, searing her skin.

"Do you like the pizza?" Luke wondered what had happened now. If it was a normal companionable silence he would have left it alone. But it wasn't. Tension emanated from her…as uncomfortable as steel wool under one's skin.

"I haven't had pizza for ages, but it tastes wonderful."

She was playing with her piece, the mechanical motions of her jaw belying her words.

"If you don't like it, say so, and I can fix you an omelet." Luke put his hand on hers to stop her lifting the slice to her mouth. The cry of pain startled him as much as it did her.

"What is it?"

Rachel's hand was behind her back. Like a child her rounded eyes relayed a distracting measure of fear and guilt. Gordie looked like that when he found something he knew he wasn't going to be allowed to play with. Gently, Luke grasped her arm and brought the hand out. The sharpness of his indrawn breath spliced the tense silence hovering around them. Three angry purple welts marred the softness of the skin on the back of her hand.

"When did this happen?"

Her hand seemed to shrink inside his as if wanting to minimize the area of contact.

"Earlier today." The rasp was back in her voice. "It's nothing. I wasn't paying attention."

Why on earth was she looking like a whipped dog?

"The oven," Luke surmised correctly. "Dinner. That's how you got burned, wasn't it?"

"Yes. It's nothing," Rachel said quickly. "I'm just not used to the oven. I was clumsy."

And he had assumed that she could handle anything. Cursing his preoccupation with his work he demanded, "Have you put anything on it?"

"I ran some cold water over it."

"That's why you don't have any blisters, I guess, but you need something for the pain."

Disappearing into the bathroom, he returned with a tube. Cradling her hand in his, he smoothed the cream over the area. Rachel stared at her hand. It was lost in Luke's large one. For all its size, his touch was gentle. She had to fight the urge to raise his hand and bury her face in it.

"Let Theresa fix the evening meals in future."

How could he have let her struggle with dinner? He should have mentioned the pizza earlier. Luke didn't realize the anger he felt at himself had escaped into his voice.

"All right. I'm sorry to be such a nuisance." The crack in her voice brought his head up. Her chin wobbled but evidently she hadn't finished what she wanted to say. Her laugh, meant he supposed to be self-deprecatory, hurt like whiskey poured on a wound. "I'm a klutz in the kitchen. I think I've ruined a baking pan. It will be easier all around if I don't attempt to develop my culinary talents at your expense."

Luke looked down at the bent head. It was either that or let her see the blaze of fury in his eyes. Who or what had given Rachel such an inferiority complex? Right now he would give away one of his Thoroughbred stallions for a few moments with the person responsible for her insecurities.

"I don't give a damn about the expense," he said brusquely, "just about your well-being." Luke couldn't help the sternness in his tone. Any minute now he was going to abandon convincing her with words and kiss some sense into her. "You can burn every pan in the kitchen if it makes you happy, but the next time you're hurt, I want to know right away. Understood?" A hand tipped her chin up.

Her eyes glistening, Rachel looked into the flame warmed navy depths, at odds with the stern set of Luke's mouth. He sounded strange, as if he had a right to say what he just had...as if he cared. A solitary silver tear overflowed. Luke's thumb caught it, swept it aside.

Rachel's chin wobbled but she held his gaze. "I'm afraid I'm not good at anything except relief work."

"Nobody's perfect," he said brusquely. "I bet not one of us on the Diamond Bar can do the kind of work you're an expert at. I've seen strong men pass out at the sight of blood."

She smiled, but he saw the you-don't-have-to-say-things-like-this look in her eyes. She thought he was just being kind? For the first time in his life, Luke understood what it really meant to be frazzled.

The silence lengthened and Rachel became aware of feeling that time had stilled, as if for something important. Was Luke going to lecture her on her responsibility to herself? The man had plenty to do without having to take care of her, as well. Hannah had shown her the medicine cabinet. She should have tended to her own hand instead of coming across as a helpless female again.

Luke cupped her face in his large warm hands and, startled, she looked at him. "Listen to me, Rae," he said seriously. "You don't have to prove anything to anyone here. That includes me. No one expects Superwoman. We like you just the way you are."

The world receded as he filled her senses. The touch of his mouth was like a butterfly caress at first. It skimmed her lips, then hovered and finally settled. After the first start of surprise Rachel relaxed, giving in to the warm undertow. Luke's gentle siege parted her lips, made her want more. She pressed herself into the solid wall of his chest and was held as if she'd finally come home.

Time raced on, unnoticed.

Rachel didn't hear the soft tap on the door. She was immersed in the feeling this had happened before...that she wasn't a stranger to these feelings, that on a previous occasion Luke had kissed her, held her and she had found peace.

The chill of disappointment as Luke put her from him made her shiver. The sound of the door opening snapped her mind to attention, as Angela entered through the back door with her father close behind.

"Temperature's dropping fast."

Rachel was grateful for the way Luke stood between her and Juan and Angela, giving her a minute to collect herself.

Juan was saying something about Theresa's rheumatism acting up, which meant they were in for a cold spell. Angela carried her overnight bag into the guest room.

"Would you like some pizza?" Rachel asked shyly.

Juan smiled at her. "No thank you. We have just eaten. Perhaps another night, you and Luke will join us for tacos? Marie will sit with Gordie."

"Would I have to bring my own fire extinguisher along?" She smiled mischievously at Juan. There was something in the manager's manner that reminded her of Tom Atwell. Warm, friendly, undemanding.

Juan threw his head back and roared with laughter. "I see Hannah has warned you about us. She hasn't forgotten the time we gave her our homemade salsa full of hot serrano peppers." He turned to Luke. "It was soon after she and Carlos were married. Hannah kept insisting she liked hot food. Theresa took her word for it and cooked a special meal for them. One bite and we thought Hannah would go up in flames." Juan chuckled again, then said, "Don't worry. We will have some not too hot for you."

"I'll look forward to it."

"If you have time," Juan said to Luke almost apologetically, "we could talk about Diamond Pride. Mr. Callaghan called again at five this evening. He's very anxious to finalize matters."

"Come into the study. Excuse us," Luke said to Rachel. "This won't take long."

The sound of the study door closing galvanized Rachel into action. Picking up her plate she glanced at the teenager who'd switched the television on. "I'm going to bed now. It's been a long day. Good night."

"Good night." Angela's voice was absent, her imagination already captured by a woman in evening dress screaming that she wanted a divorce.

Rachel shut the door of her room and leaned against it. Luke. She touched her lips. He'd kissed her, held her as if it meant something. As if *she* meant something. Was it just a gesture as insubstantial as the moonbeams trailing across her bed, or had those moments meant something to him, as well?

In the week she'd been here, Rachel had learned Luke wasn't a man who said or did what he didn't mean.

She fell asleep with a smile in her heart.

* * *

The smell of frying bacon woke her at eight. Jumping up, Rachel grabbed the velour robe Luke had bought for her and hurled herself into the kitchen.

Gordie was in his high chair, playing with a spoon. Luke was by the stove. A maroon-and-cream sweater strained to confine his upper body, his lean lithe hips were encased in cream corduroys. Rachel knew the apron he was wrapped in had Kiss the Cook emblazoned on the front.

"Hi! Sleep well?" His eyes trailed over her from top to bottom in a leisurely scrutiny. The responsive surge of adrenaline in Rachel's body brought her wide-awake. Gordie banged his spoon on his tray and she bent to kiss him, glad of an excuse to hide her flushed face.

"I overslept," she confessed softly. "You should have woken me."

"Why?" Luke asked matter-of-factly. "You need your sleep. Gordie and I always share the morning hours."

*Could she apply for the night hours if there was a vacancy?* The thought shocked Rachel into absolute stillness. She put a hand up to her head.

"Rachel? Is something wrong?" He reached for her, but she moved quickly, putting Gordie and the high chair between them.

"No. Nothing's wrong," she said. Gently prying Gordie's fingers loose from around the middle finger of her left hand, she gave him his small silver spoon to hold instead. "I think I'll have a shower right away. I won't be long."

Trudging to the bathroom she put a hand up to her head again. Was she crazy? Fantasizing about Luke was like deliberately stepping into crocodile infested waters.

Under the shower, she thought of the men in her life. She'd had a few offers abroad from men who were lonely, men who wanted to forget the miseries of what they saw, what they dealt with, and from men who were just plain hungry for a female body. She hadn't accepted any because not one of them had touched her soul.

Rachel lathered her hair, trying to wash thoughts of Luke out but for the first time in the longest while, her mind couldn't control what her body was feeling. A kiss that left a warm glow was one thing, but this urge to fling herself into Luke's arms everytime he looked at her amazed her. She couldn't understand why this had to happen now. Things were complicated enough already.

Tilting her head, Rachel allowed water to cascade over her and wash away all the soapy residue, willing it to remove the strange impulses crowding her brain, as well.

## Chapter Seven

We're going to pick out a tree today," Luke announced halfway through breakfast.

The fierce protectiveness that had welled up at the sight of Rachel's freshly scrubbed face, the trembling pink lips unadorned by lipstick, surprised Luke. She'd responded to him like a moth to the flame last night. This morning, straight out of bed, she'd looked one hundred percent adorable. If she hadn't bolted, he would have kissed her again.

Rachel Carstairs didn't have an iota of self-preservation. He'd sensed the surrender and the yearning in her kisses. And right now, she was as ready for the rest as Gordie was for steak. It was up to him to see she didn't get in over her head.

Rachel stared up at him. "A tree? A Christmas tree?"

Luke nodded. "Chris and Rob would want Gordie's first Christmas to be special. We'll have a tree and lights but not the usual parties. Dad's followed my advice and booked on a cruise through the holidays. It's something he enjoys doing and hopefully it will help him through this period. He offered to come here but his arthritis will only get worse. I told him we'd visit him in Arizona as soon as he gets back in the New Year."

When Luke used *we* was it just a figure of speech, or had she deliberately been included? A chill chased down Rachel's spine and she trembled as she recalled the kiss last night. Had it just been an experiment, or was it one of those "I'm serious" ones. Lying awake, wondering half the night hadn't provided Rachel with an answer.

"Will you be ready to leave in an hour?" The lifted eyebrow told her he was aware she was daydreaming, and Rachel felt the warm color seep into her face. "We'll take a picnic lunch and return about four."

"What about your work?"

The day had assumed rainbow hues suddenly. A picnic with Luke. Hours alone with him. A pulse throbbed in her throat. She wanted to go. She wanted not to.

"All done. I hit the Save button at three this morning and punched the messages into the modem at work. I'm free for the rest of the week to give you a hand with Gordie."

Rachel wasn't sure all that freedom was such a good thing—for her at any rate.

Theresa, Juan's wife, arrived promptly at eight. David, her youngest, was better today and back in school.

"He loves wading in the stream near the house and it's been so cold lately," she told them both, as she picked up Gordie for a hug and a kiss. "He must have caught a chill."

Luke told her about the tree-cutting expedition and she nodded. "It's a nice day for an outing. It's supposed to go up to the mid-sixties today. Don't you worry about a thing. Marie and I will manage fine."

"I could stay back..." Rachel offered, surprised by the rebellion that surged through her at the thought.

"Of course not," Theresa said, looking amazed. "You need to be out in the fresh air. Marie will be here by nine and this is my only chance of some time alone with Gordie."

When they were ready to leave, Luke picked up a picnic basket from the counter. When had he had time to pack that? Between giving Gordie his breakfast and making theirs?

He didn't miss the lingering look Rachel gave Gordie as the latter's face scrunched up in protest at their departure. The ten-month-old knew he was being left behind.

"Don't worry," Luke assured her, giving Gordie a hug and a kiss on the cheek. "These are his crocodile tears. They don't last two minutes. He loves Theresa."

"Maybe I should stay and help? Theresa's rheumatism—"

"Is fine," Luke cut in firmly. "I asked her about it and she said she can manage fine with Marie. Hannah called while you were in the shower and suggested we defrost one of her frozen casseroles for dinner. Theresa doesn't have to do a thing except watch Gordie."

Placing an arm on her shoulders, he turned Rachel toward the door. "You deserve a day off after being such a brick yesterday. Come on."

He wouldn't let her carry the ax or the picnic basket. She finally managed to get the blanket from him and hugged it to her. It did nothing to smother the budding excitement that made her feel like a diver poised on the edge of a cliff.

A half an hour later they were by the little grove. Luke paused for a moment to look around and, taking a deep breath of pine-scented air, Rachel did the same. The hills had a special softness today.

"Watch your step," Luke warned. "The trail gets steeper after this and the pine needles make it slippery."

Rachel looked up. The path wound upward and disappeared. She wet her lips and hesitated.

"Not afraid of heights are you?"

"No. It's not that." She was just afraid, period. Afraid of the way she was feeling, of the fact that strange emotions were making inroads in the carefully banked control she'd always counted on. The path she was on emotionally seemed to lead to a future where she had no control. And losing control meant leaving herself open to pain.

"Let's go then, or we'll be walking back in the dark."

Luke set his pace by hers, resting often so she could look at the view and catch her breath. When they reached the glade of evergreens, Rachel squinted up at the sun.

"Eleven o'clock," she announced. "It took us only forty-five minutes to get here. I thought it was much longer."

Luke looked surprised, checked his watch and said, "You're right. Where did you learn to tell time like that?" He'd seen her bare wrists too often not to know she didn't own a watch.

"Abroad." Rachel smiled self-consciously. "One of the cooks at the main MRA camp had every single meal ready on time. He taught me how to tell time by the position of the sun."

Luke took the blanket from her and spread it on the ground. Rachel sat down cross-legged as he began to rifle through the picnic basket.

"You really like your work, don't you?"

Whenever she talked about her life abroad her face took on a special softness.

"Yes." Her eyes took on a serious look, as if she was seeing private pictures he had no access to. "Very much."

"What made you decide to go so far away? You must have been a kid when you left."

"Eighteen," Rachel said reflectively, plucking a blade of grass and chewing on one end. She didn't answer the first part of his question.

"Why did you go, Rae?" Luke persisted after waiting a while. "Most eighteen-year-olds are thinking about college, jobs, having fun, fast cars, dates, clothes..."

She'd turned eighty the day her mother had left. "The work appealed to me. I felt I would fill a need."

There it was, in a nutshell, but he wanted more. "Didn't your parents mind? I remember Chris mentioning once that you were an only child."

It seemed as if a cold front moved into the gray eyes that gazed into the distance and Luke felt a twinge of prescience. He could tell just by looking at her that it had been *because* of her family she'd decided to go abroad.

She shrugged, trying to sound casual. "It's what I wanted to do."

Turning to the basket, Luke took out one of Hannah's fruitcakes and undoing the brandy-soaked cheesecloth it was wrapped in, he cursed himself for stirring up painful memories for Rachel. She'd looked so alive on the way here, laughing out loud as he had told her about some of the misadventures they'd had on the farm over the years.

Deliberately, he embarked on another tale as he unpacked the food, trying to restore her earlier mood.

There were turkey sandwiches and some ham rolls, as well as a fresh salad in a plastic container and Luke's favorite blue cheese dressing.

Rachel bit into a ham roll. "Mmm, this is so good."

"Theresa only brings them over when Hannah is away. Hannah's very possessive about who feeds her family."

Luke saw her reach for another roll, glad he'd managed to take her mind off whatever troubled secret her past held. Already she looked different from the woman he'd seen outside the courtroom. She didn't pick at her food these days and her face glowed with color. She smiled readily, and had lost the air of a doe waiting for a panther to pounce.

"You don't much care for salad, do you?" he asked, smothering crisp lettuce and tomatoes with blue cheese.

Rachel stopped with her roll halfway to her mouth. "It's not that I don't like salad. It's just that we never ate any raw greens or vegetables abroad. It was safer just to eat cooked vegetables."

Finishing her ham roll, she took the turkey sandwich Luke held out to her. Her eyes were on the cake. "That isn't one of Hannah's fruitcakes, is it?" she asked.

"It is."

"Hannah said they had to remain wrapped in the brandy-soaked muslin for a month before they would be ready. Won't she be upset?"

"No. We always take one of her cakes when we go on our cutting-the-tree picnic."

He looked at his plate as if he'd suddenly lost all taste for his food. Rachel knew Luke was remembering other times when he'd come up here with his family. Happier times.

"When were these trees planted?" The need to distract Luke, ease his pain, supplanted her usual shyness.

"Five years ago. We plant a new area each year. Great Grandpa Jasper told his son, my Grandfather Robert, that the land was a gift from God that had to be preserved as close to its original state as possible. It's become a family tradition to do as much as we can to keep the sanctity of nature intact, mate it with progress in a way that doesn't cause harm."

That Luke was a giver Rachel already knew. That he was a man who would always give more than he took, she was beginning to find out.

"This whole area is beautiful."

"Tell me about your work," Luke asked abruptly. He wanted to know more about her, get inside her thoughts and find out what had made her the way she was.

"I didn't do much. I was sort of a medical assistant cum general dogsbody."

"Who delivered babies by herself, gave injections and even pulled teeth?"

Rachel's eyes widened. "Who told you that?"

"I heard all about the talk Jason asked you to give the staff last Wednesday night after you treated Mojo. He told me it was a record turnout."

As she busied herself pouring tea, Luke thought back to the evening he'd mentioned. He'd been busy at his computer and when he'd finally surfaced for a cup of tea, Hannah had told him where Rachel was. He'd reached the old barn that had been converted to a recreation hall in time to hear the tail end of her talk.

"It isn't glamorous and it doesn't pay well," she'd concluded, "but it has its own rewards."

"Can anyone join MRA?"

The question from one of the younger men was answered with confidence. "Yes, but relief work needs a special kind of strength—mental and physical."

Luke knew she had plenty of both. He just puzzled over how it had been forged in one so young.

Another hand shot up. "Didn't you miss your life here, terribly?"

Rachel turned toward the speaker. "No." She had said it with quiet conviction and the fact she didn't elaborate made it all the more forceful.

The expressions on the people's faces told Luke she'd captured their attention. He'd looked at her face, flushed with the intensity of her feelings, with love for her work, and felt fear thread his being. Was what he had to offer her enough to keep her here? She had no use for money, which left him with only one card to play. Love.

Later, Jason had mentioned to him that the staff were going to start a collection for MRA. Word had gotten around and Hattie Gorkie, one of the wives, had invited Rachel to talk to her craft club about her work in Bangladesh.

"Were you happy out there, Rae?"

"Why do you keep calling me that?"

"Rae?" Luke held her gaze steadily. "Because I think it suits you. I looked up your name in a book of baby names and Rachel means ewe lamb, but Rae spelled R-A-E means doe and that's what you remind me of. A gentle, beautiful doe."

She swallowed hard. Had anyone told this man he had poetry in his soul? Any defense she mustered would be useless against it.

"You didn't answer my question," Luke reminded her stubbornly. "Were you happy there?"

"Very."

Luke could tell from the look on her face that she wasn't going to say more on the subject.

"Tell me about the worst thing that happened to you, out there," he coaxed.

She didn't even have to think about it. "It was in Bangladesh, just before I left. The floods had destroyed almost everything and we were in this tiny village giving cholera shots. I was working alone with the children and Tom was attending a breech birth, when a whole riverbank slipped away in front of our eyes." Rachel swallowed, her eyes filming at the memory. "A woman had been washing a few rags near the edge and she slipped right into the swirling muddy water, screaming. I found her clinging to a root and managed to get a grip on her wrists. I didn't know if I could hold on long enough, but suddenly Tom was there and some other men. They pulled her out just in time."

The nightmare. This explained it.

"What was the best thing that happened to you?" prompted Luke.

Rachel's brow wrinkled in thought, then she smiled. "In the middle of my second year abroad, we were working in a village trying to teach the people about nutrition and disease prevention. There were just the two of us then, Tom and I, because it was considered an easy assignment." She chuckled over her memories and the sound gladdened Luke's heart. "Anyway, after we'd been there a week, the headman wanted to know if Tom and I were going to be married soon. When Tom told him we weren't, there was a great deal of head shaking and whispering. The next morning Tom came out of his hut to find two oxen, one goat and five chickens outside.

"This is the dowry for the woman," the headman told him. "She is skinny, but soft-spoken and will bear you many sons. Will you have her now?" Rachel laughed at the memory of Tom's face.

"How did Dr. Atwell get out of that one?"

"He said something about not being able to marry me, because he was already betrothed to another woman, but he'd taken it upon himself to find a husband for me among the other workers. The headman wasn't too happy, but he had to accept that. When we left he reminded Tom that the dowry would be there any time it was needed. A year later we were at a neighboring village, and he sent a man over to find out if I was still unmarried and to remind us of the waiting dowry.''

The woman who'd heard him mention the price of his stallions without flicking an eyelash had eyes filled with tears over the memory of plain, honest caring.

Her sandwich was gone, Luke noticed. Talking seemed to have given her a keen appetite.

Rachel took the plate Luke held out to her. The generous portion of fruitcake he'd cut her looked tempting. The first bite proved it. ''Mmm. This is heavenly. Hannah could market it and make a fortune.''

''She and her sister do.'' Luke named the brand it was marketed under. ''Hannah has quite a bit of her own money. What I give her is nothing compared to what she does for us. It's the same with all the Rodriguez family, but after the accident, nothing would do except Theresa should come up to the house every day and help Hannah. I protested but Juan told me to let her be. It was the only way she could come to terms with her grief.''

''Chris and Rob were well-loved, weren't they?''

Luke nodded. ''Yes. There are people here who've seen Rob and me grow up. Juan was Rob's godfather. Chris found her own place in their hearts with her warm nature, her capacity for caring about everyone she met.'' His eyes darkened reflectively. ''She was so much fun, always teasing me about getting married and making her an aunt, giving Gordie some cousins to play with.''

''Does your father like Arizona?'' It was time to change the subject. She wanted to dispel the shadow of sadness in his eyes.

''My mother died three years ago and after that he lost interest in the farm. Dr. Kenton suggested a change would help his arthritis and help him stop grieving for my mother.

He's made a few friends in Arizona, has a small stable and rides every day. He visits us twice a year.''

"He isn't in a home, then?''

Luke looked surprised. ''Oh, no. He has a small house with a couple of acres land in what is called a retirement community, but he's very independent.''

Life, Rachel knew, followed a pattern of regeneration. Birth, death, suffering, joy, were all part of the pattern. When Luke brought his bride to the Diamond Bar, happiness would reign again. Rachel wondered about the kind of woman he would choose. Someone like his mother, who'd grown up in these hills, or someone like Chris, warm, wonderful, who would bring sunshine into his life and Gordie's. Rachel blinked. For some reason her mind refused to supply her with a composite sketch of Luke's future wife.

Luke took off his jacket, bundled it under his head and stretched out. His eyes closed and she looked at the sweep of his dark lashes against his bronzed cheeks. He looked strangely vulnerable like that.

"You aren't going to fall asleep now after that big meal, are you?'' she asked.

He opened one lazy eye. "I can't cut down a tree right this minute. Why don't you lie down, as well?''

Rachel looked at the arm extended to pillow her head, at the length of Luke's hard frame. Preposterous ideas flooded her brain. Willful, insistent, demanding. She jumped up as if she'd just seen a rattlesnake. "I'm going for a short walk.''

"Okay,'' he said comfortably, "but remember we have to walk back, too. I have to manage the tree...I won't be able to carry you.''

Rachel didn't go far. Out of sight, she stopped and looked around. From here she had a clear view of the ocean, could even see the waves as they flung themselves on shore. If she closed her eyes, she could recall the sensation of being carried by Luke. His arms had cradled her to his strength. In her present picture he didn't leave her on the bed. She held her hand out to him and his eyes changed as he looked down at her, the look in them promising her the happiness she'd never before let herself dream about.

Rachel's eyes flew open and she raised a hand to her head. The brandy in that cake must be affecting her. It was the only explanation for her hallucinations.

Luke was fast asleep when she got back. Stretching out beside him without touching him, Rachel told herself she would get up in a minute and closed her eyes.

Gordie was patting her cheek with one arm as she gave him his bottle, saying her name softly. She frowned. There was something wrong with her dream. Gordie couldn't say her name yet. Opening one eye she saw Luke's face directly over hers, suffused with an incredible tenderness. He didn't belong in her dream.

"Go 'way," she said indistinctly, "ate too much. Having bad dreams."

"Thanks a lot." Luke's laugh seemed to vibrate through her. "I've been called a lot of things but never a bad dream."

Watching her sleep he remembered her first night at the Diamond Bar. She'd burrowed into his arms seeking warmth then. The need to hold her again spiraled into an ache within him.

Rachel reached up and rubbed her eyes. Finally she opened them. "This isn't a dream?"

"No." Just to prove it he leaned over her, intending merely to brush his lips against hers. She held him with her quick response. Her lips parted eagerly. A moment later his chest rested against the softness of her breasts and he was trailing kisses down the side of her face, returning again and again to drink of the sweetness of her mouth. She whimpered whenever he pulled away from her lips, the little mews igniting a fierce hunger. When they broke for air he rolled onto his side, keeping her within the circle of his arms. He had to maintain control. If he took her now, he would lose her completely.

Her eyes were still closed, so he couldn't tell what she was thinking. Her flushed face and the trembling softness of her lips held the stamp of passion and Luke stroked her head, marveling at the silky softness of her hair. Her scent infiltrated his nostrils reminding him of scented, summer roses.

"Rae..." he said at last, his voice slightly husky with emotion. "I don't want you to leave yet."

Her immediate stillness warned of his mistake. Easing herself out of his arms she sat up and put her arms around herself, keeping her back to him.

"Rachel?"

"Shouldn't we get our tree? It's going to be dark pretty soon." She stood up and dusted off her jeans, the hoarseness in her voice the only sign of her tension.

That was it? He had as good as told her he loved her and all she could think of was getting back? He wasn't about to let her ignore real, honest emotion.

He got to his feet in a lithe movement and stood facing her.

Rachel's heart sank. He wasn't going to let it go. When had she fallen in love with Luke? That first day in the courtroom? When he'd carried her to the bathroom? When she'd seen the way he was with Gordie? She couldn't separate knowing him from loving him.

"I...I don't know what to say."

"Try...I want to stay, Luke," he suggested.

Rachel cleared her throat painfully. "It wouldn't be any use. I've never been any good at personal relations. I don't want to hurt either you or Gordie."

"How could you do that?" Luke asked reasonably.

"I don't know." Rachel shook her head, feeling helpless, feeling trapped. How did one translate into words her fear. The fear that no one who had ever known her had loved her? The fear that if she let someone love her pain would happen again.

Her parents were proof of that. Her mother had left one day while Rachel was at school. And only that morning she'd made her pancakes for breakfast and talked about a visit to the zoo. She hadn't even left a note. All her father had told her was that her mother wasn't coming back—ever. Life had never been the same again. Day after empty day her father's changed attitude toward her had cemented the belief that it was all her fault.

Rachel's hands clenched the tufts of grass on either side of her.

"Rae." Flinching from the hand Luke put on her shoulder, she didn't see his eyes darken to the color of sapphires. "I won't rush you. Let's get used to the idea of being friends first before we explore our feelings for each other."

"My feelings aren't involved." Her lips seemed to have swollen to twice their size, making the lie all the more difficult to utter. "I'm sorry, Luke."

That was it? She'd decided it wouldn't work and nothing else mattered? Anger blazed a trail through him and he acted on impulse.

"What's this, then?" He placed his hands on her shoulders, uncertain whether to shake the truth out of her, or to kiss her till she admitted it.

The flash flood of apprehension in her eyes changed his course. Hauling her to his chest, he rocked her slightly saying nothing. The spark of anger that had almost fanned it-self into something ugly wasn't like him. Neither was losing control. Luke called himself every name he could think of. And then he repeated them all.

He didn't want to force anything out of her. Not even the truth about her feelings. When she cared enough, admitting it would come naturally. A gift, even the gift of love, didn't mean a thing unless it was given freely.

The pounding of her heart reminded him of waves crashing on a rocky shore. He held her for his sake more than her own, till they were both calmer.

Rachel's eyes flooded. She would never be able to fool Luke. Her kisses had been a dead giveaway. Yet they hadn't changed a thing. The gap between her feelings and her thoughts still yawned like a chasm. One without a bridge.

She stirred in his arms and he released her immediately.

The sight of her face made Luke feel like kicking himself. Her shuttered expression reminded him of the first time he'd seen her. He watched her gnaw her lower lip for a few seconds, but she didn't say a word.

Raising one hand, he brushed the wisp of hair off her forehead and then traced his knuckles down the side of her face and watched the color return.

"We'll work things out. Don't worry," he said gruffly.

Why was he talking to her as if the rest of their lives was a foregone conclusion? Rachel knew one thing for certain. She had to be strong. Neither he nor Gordie needed someone in their lives who'd always earned a failing grade in relations of the human kind.

She looked into Luke's eyes and was lost. She hated being cause for the concern in his eyes, the muscle throbbing in his jaw.

Luke hesitated a minute longer, then held a hand out to her. "Right now, we have a tree to get, remember?" he said cheerfully. "We have to hurry."

Bewildered, Rachel put her hand in his. How could he switch back so quickly into the role of undemanding friend? Why wasn't he angry with her? Men she'd barely known had sulked for days when she'd refused to meet them after work.

Following him through the rows of orderly evergreens, Rachel stopped when he did.

"This one?"

Luke pointed to one barely three feet high. It looked too small to Rachel. Somehow she'd imagined a larger tree, one that would do justice to the cathedral ceiling in the living room. Her gaze veered to the right to one that stood eight feet tall.

"That one?" Luke walked over to it, examined the branches and lifted the ax.

"Wait," Rachel called out, "I'm not sure. I don't know a thing about trees. Let's take this one." She put a hand out to the one that Luke had picked first.

"Sweetheart," he said, leaning on his ax, "I want to get this one now."

His glance mocked her. *See?* it said, *it isn't as hard as you think. All it takes is compromise. Give and take.* As she looked at him, Luke's eyes darkened in the way that warned he meant to kiss her. He took a step forward. Rachel panicked. One more kiss like the last and she wouldn't even be able to spell her own name, let alone make plans to return to Bangladesh. Stepping back, she stopped when a branch brushed her spine. "I'll pack the picnic basket while you cut down the tree. That way we'll save time," she said, fleeing immediately.

Luke hefted the trunk of the tree to rest against one broad shoulder, letting the rest of the tree drag behind him. In his other hand he held the ax. Rachel carried the empty picnic basket and blanket simply because she'd gotten there first and refused to give them up.

They walked home in silence for the most part, each preoccupied with their own thoughts.

They were on the home hill when Luke said casually, "You know, Rae, one of these days, you're going to have to stop running and face those fears we talked about. All I'm asking is that when the time comes, you give yourself a fair deal."

## Chapter Eight

Marie had just taken over with Gordie, and Rachel was free for the rest of the morning. It was always difficult to leave Gordie, but usurping all the other women's time with the baby wouldn't be fair, either. This way, the degree to which Gordie would miss her, would be cushioned at least.

Coming out of the sun room she paused a minute to admire the decorated tree in the corner of the living room. The fresh scent permeated the whole house. Gordie had everyone in splits of laughter by mimicking her deep breaths and following it up with an *Aah* of appreciation.

Angela and her younger brother, David, had decorated the tree after school the day before. The white doves and the silver tinsel enhanced the majesty of the fir with their pristine simplicity. Already Christmas presents had mysteriously appeared under the tree, adding to the magic of the season.

"Do you know where Luke is?" she asked Theresa casually.

He hadn't appeared at breakfast and she'd simply assumed he was working in his study. It was unusual for him not to come out for his usual cups of tea.

"I haven't seen him since he put Gordie in his crib this morning," Theresa said quietly.

For the first time that day Rachel became aware of how strained the older woman looked.

"Do you think he might be at the farm?"

Theresa thought for a minute. "No. I don't think so. There are too many people there. Rob would have gone there if he was upset. He always needed sheer physical labor if something was bothering him, but Luke is different. He searches for the quiet places."

"Is something wrong?"

Theresa looked out of the kitchen window. "Today would have been Robbie's thirty-fourth birthday."

"Where can I find Luke?" Rachel couldn't keep the breathless urgency out of her voice. Theresa would work out her grief scouring the kitchen and going down to the mission in Santa Barbara to recite a rosary, but the fact that Luke had disappeared like a wounded animal worried Rachel tremendously. To run and hide, his pain had to be soul deep. She had to go to him.

Theresa said slowly, "Do you remember the spot where he took you for the Christmas tree? Past the area there is a trail that goes right to the top of Jasper's mountain." Her lips trembled before she tightened them and went on. "It's where the family graves are. I think he might be there."

It seemed a long way when one went up the path alone. In spite of a jacket and her sweater, Rachel shivered. The wind had lowered the temperature considerably and the overcast sky seemed to fit the solemnity of the day. Past the evergreens where they'd picnicked the path grew steeper. Doubts set in as she huffed and puffed her way to the top.

Was she doing the right thing seeking Luke out like this? Instinct urged this course of action and she'd obeyed blindly.

Rachel paused on the edge of the clearing in surprise. Walled in by a six-foot-evergreen hedge on three sides, the clearing was huge. December roses were in full bloom everywhere, the riot of color suggesting life everlasting instead of an ending. If it weren't for the gravestones, she would have taken the spot for some sort of enchanted garden. Rachel's gaze wandered from the oldest to the newest and the largest in white marble. A single grave. It seemed right that Chris and Rob hadn't been parted even in the choice of their final resting place. The fresh flowers covering the grave told her others had paid their respects here today.

Luke sat with his back against a tree, looking away from the graves, out into the distance. One long leg was bent at the knee, the other stretched out. One hand aimlessly picked up tiny stones and threw them at some distant object in the horizon while his eyes stared unseeingly ahead. Emotion so thick she could almost cut it with a knife surrounded him.

Rachel came up quietly behind him. There was no need to say anything. Luke hadn't turned his head but Rachel knew he sensed her presence. She looked out at the horizon. This had to be the highest point in the Diamond Bar. From here one could get an eagle's-eye view of almost all the land, and way out in the distance a clear view of the ocean.

Instinct told her Jasper Summers had stood on this spot and been captured by the wild beauty that surrounded him. Here he must have realized that he'd found his gold vein after all, and asked that his body be laid to rest in the spot where he'd first felt a passion for the place.

Rachel sat down. Her legs ached with the climb and nervousness seemed to infuse them with what was becoming a familiar weakness whenever Luke was nearby.

"Rae."

"Hello, Luke."

She could see he hadn't shaved, that his eyes were sunken. His lips were white, a warning that physically he wasn't doing to well, either. When had he last eaten? Grief submerged physical needs. Hunger intensified suffering. It was a vicious circle. Luke's pain was the kind that needed more than medical knowledge and skill to deal with it. More than an impulse. Nervously Rachel wet her lips and waited.

A scene exploded on her mental screen. Bangladesh. A funeral. She'd been on the outskirts of the crowd watching the mourners beat their chests and wail aloud. That kind of outburst was better than this silent suffering.

Had Luke ever taken the time to grieve for Rob and Chris? Always the comforter, never the comforted, had he overlooked his own need to mourn?

Rachel thought of the strength she'd drawn on since the first moment she had seen him, of the way he was with Hannah and Theresa. Calm, gently teasing, talking to them about his work and the farm, listening to them go over their day, as if he sensed the well of loneliness Rob and Chris's deaths had plunged them into. As if he wanted to make up to them for it.

Anyone could provide for another materially, but Luke nurtured souls.

Rachel hauled in a deep breath, let it out slowly and lifted her chin.

"You shouldn't have come. It's cold."

"I know." Rubbing her hands together she blew on them. Four and a half years in a warm climate had thinned her blood. She huddled deeper inside her jacket, placing her numb hands under her armpits.

"Come here." Luke held each hand between both of his and rubbed briskly. Rachel struggled with the desire to lift his hands to her face. The sudden flush that swept her body at the thought shamed her. She was here to give if she could, not take. Gently she removed her hands from his grasp and reached for the bag slung on her shoulders. "I brought some lunch."

The boiled egg sandwiches were Luke's favorite. Theresa hadn't said a word as she'd watched Rachel make them and then wrap a generous slab of Hannah's fruitcake in foil. She'd merely added a thermos of herbal tea and told her to dress warmly.

Luke didn't say a word, either. Rachel consoled herself silence was better than an outright denial that he needed food.

"They're not very good," she hurried on, hating to trick him, but desperate enough to try anything. "I won't blame you for not finishing even one. You'd think I could at least make a decent sandwich by now."

It worked. He looked at her, reached for one of the sandwiches and said, "You did well with the quiche the other night."

Watching him take his first bite Rachel said, "Only because Theresa was right there telling me exactly what to do."

She kept up a flood of small talk, glad to see the gauntness leave his face as he ate, putting another sandwich into his hands as soon as he finished the first. By the time the cake was gone, his lips had resumed their normal, healthy color.

Rachel got to her feet brushing the crumbs from her clothes. She'd eaten a whole sandwich herself before remembering she didn't care for this particular filling.

"Gordie must be up from his nap by now. I'd better be getting back."

She held her breath. Would Luke come with her or would he choose to linger here with his memories? She'd just tended to his body. The way to his soul Rachel wasn't sure she would find so easily.

Her luck held. He stirred and got to his feet. "I'll walk back with you."

They didn't say much on the way back but close to the house Luke cleared his throat and said, "Thanks, Rae."

As soon as they got back Rachel gave Marie the rest of the afternoon off. Step two of her impromptu plan was about to go into action. When Luke came out of his bedroom, shaved and freshly showered, Rachel held Gordie out to him.

"Would you keep an eye on him for me?" she asked. "Marie wasn't feeling too well, so I sent her home to rest. I'm going to try out a new recipe for a lemon cake that requires all my concentration."

That part was plausible, anyway. Every recipe, even boiling eggs, needed her total concentration.

Nap-refreshed, Gordie's demands would keep Luke too busy to brood. She watched him tuck his nephew under his arm and go toward his study. Tiptoeing to the study door a while later, the sound of Gordie's chuckles informed her that they were mock wrestling on the carpet. Smiling, Rachel hurried back to sprinkle some flour on the counter and leave some lemon rinds there as well, wondering what else went into a lemon cake. If Luke ever thought to ask about the cake she could always say it had gone the way of her other disasters: feed for the garbage disposal.

While Luke gave Gordie his dinner, Rachel made a great show of cleaning up after herself. Hannah's chicken casserole was being reheated in the oven and Rachel hoped the aroma would entice Luke into the kitchen. It didn't.

He bathed Gordie, tucked him into his crib for the night and went back into his study, firmly shutting the door. Rachel waited half an hour before she went into her plan of action. Picking up the tray she'd prepared she squared her shoulders.

The room was in darkness when she pushed it open with her foot, the wedge of light coming in through the open door the only source of illumination. Luke's chair was facing the large window. He didn't even turn his head when she set the tray down.

Rachel swallowed and came up behind his chair. This wasn't interference, she told herself. Not when his pain needed to be assuaged. Not when her heart ached to ease it.

Gently, she put her hands on his shoulders and began kneading, moving up to the muscles of his neck. Iron would have been more malleable.

"Tell me about Rob."

The words were stiff at first, but slowly the tempo picked up, the sentences became smoother. Luke described escapade after escapade, surprised to find himself laughing over the mischief they'd gotten into as boys. Then later there had been girls and college. A deep and abiding sibling friendship had enriched their lives. They had always been able to talk to each other, count on each other.

When Luke stopped talking, Rachel simply said, "Good memories are their own strength, aren't they?"

And Luke had to acknowledge they were. As he had talked he'd felt Rob's presence in the room and it had been like a shaft of sunlight aimed at his heart. Warming, healing, *erasing*.

"If it had been you, and not Rob and Chris who'd been killed," Rachel asked, going straight for the jugular, "how would you have liked to be remembered?"

He went so still she thought he wouldn't answer. Then Luke spoke softly, as if raising the curtain on a certain thought for the first time. "I would have wanted to be remembered with love, with joy."

"By the way you were in life, not the manner of your death?" Rachel prompted softly.

She didn't say anything more for quite a while. She didn't need to. A clock ticked each passing moment. She could sense the difference in Luke.

Luke looked at the tray. When had Rae stopped working on his shoulders and slipped into the chair pulled up to his desk? She'd pushed a plate toward him, nudged the wicker basket of crusty rolls in his direction but said nothing. He had done justice to the meal while he'd talked. Now he had to do justice to his brother's memory.

Rae was right. There was so much happiness packed into his memories of Rob, so much to hold on to. As reason drowned the pain, Luke knew he would never again allow bitterness to cloud his memories.

The knowledge freed him from an iron ball and chain of his own making. He felt drained, refreshed, whole.

Rachel stood up and reached for the tray. Her work here was done.

Luke caught the hand she put out for the tray, meaning only to thank her. But the feel of her small wrist ignited a voracious fire inside him. With a small tug she was in his lap. He wanted her close to him, just for a few minutes, he told himself, just long enough to reassure him his angel was a flesh and blood human being.

His senses reeled under the impact of her in his arms. She fit perfectly. If she'd been stiff he would have exercised caution but she snuggled up to him like Gordie might have. Boneless, trusting, eager. The scent of crushed roses teased his nostrils and they flared as he tried to rein in desire.

"Luke?" The excitement threaded with apprehension showing on her face heightened his awareness. Her breath, warm and sweet, flirted with the muscles on his cheek.

"Thank you for helping me put things in perspective." Odd he should sound so hoarse. He didn't want to frighten her with the force of his feelings. Maybe words would help him cool off. "I had things under control till Dad called this morning. He sounded so sad, so tired. He said the greatest sorrow any man could face was to live long enough to see his children die. Something snapped in me then, and I had to get away."

"I know." She lifted her hand and for a fleeting moment rested her fingertips against his cheek. The strongest always fell the hardest. Luke had been so busy getting on with life he hadn't even realized he owed his mind time to grieve, to adjust.

Luke tensed under her touch. It was the first time Rachel had touched him like this. He looked at her and suddenly he wanted her closer. Much, much closer. Lowering his lips, he delved into the comfort she was offering so freely.

Rachel wasn't aware of threading her fingers through Luke's hair, of urging him to increase the pressure of his mouth. All she knew was every nerve in her body was straining toward him. Their clothes seemed to be in the way. She slid her hand into the neck of his shirt, splaying her fingers against his skin, exploring the satiny surface.

Luke knew it wouldn't take much to make love with her here and now, but there were too many other things to consider. Sympathy wasn't to be mistaken for love. It was part of her giving nature that she wouldn't hold anything back, wouldn't regret anything. But he would. There was more at stake here than the need to lose oneself temporarily. Rae deserved nothing less than love.

Gently he placed his hands on her upper arms, held her away. When she came to him, it would have nothing to do with sympathy or compassion.

Luke hugged her as he saw the embarrassment dawn on her face, claimed one last kiss and then put her on her feet. "I think I hear Angela in the family room."

Rachel pressed her palms against her hot cheeks to cool them. She'd latched on to his change of mood. She didn't need it spelled out to realize that she'd been a hairsbreadth away from making an utter fool of herself. "I have to check on Gordie."

She was almost at the door when Luke stopped her. Hand on the knob to keep it shut, he lifted her chin with a finger. "Rachel, don't misunderstand what just happened in here," he ordered sternly. "I want you, but when we make love it will stem only from our feelings for each other—nothing else." He watched the rich color flood her face before he said, "Loving is a celebration of a man and a woman's commitment to each other. Nothing should be allowed to mar that celebration. Not compassion, not doubts."

He opened the door for her and Rachel walked out on legs that had lost all sensation. She didn't know what she said to Angela, who fortunately was already immersed in her favorite television series.

In her room Rachel leaned against the door, pressing a hand over her heart. It was beating like a sledgehammer. Fast, furious, *excited*.

She'd thought of love—of loving—often. But never in her wildest dreams had she thought of it as a celebration. She shivered, thinking of Luke's dark eyes, the hands that were so clever. Yes, the woman Luke loved wouldn't be in any doubt that she was taking part in a celebration.

\* \* \*

Luke watched her mount Sabrina from the office window. She rode as she did so many other things—with a quiet confidence.

He thought of the way she'd felt on his lap yesterday and his eyes narrowed. If he had taken what she'd offered so readily how would she be feeling today? Or had she already decided to have an affair with him and then go back to Bangladesh, heart whole and fancy free, content with the knowledge she'd loved a man?

Juan was saying something about supplies. Luke listened absent-mindedly.

No, Rachel wasn't capable of a cold-blooded decision like that. The armor she'd donned had more cracks now than the San Andreas fault. She cared about things and people deeply. To her caring was synonymous with giving. He thought of the way she was with Gordie, the look on her face when Hannah had said her back hurt, the way she'd bullied Mojo into listening to her. Rachel Carstairs was all woman. A lifetime of loving her wouldn't be enough. The problem was to convince her of it.

"I know it's a large order," Juan said, "but at this price and if the quality is consistent with the samples we've been sent, we could be getting a real bargain."

"Umm," Luke said.

Take yesterday for instance. She'd gotten through to him as no one had since the accident that had taken Rob and Chris. But he couldn't delude himself into thinking it was because he was who he was. Rae would have done the same for anyone in his place. She had the magic of healing at her fingertips, an instinct that went beyond mere knowledge or experience. Surely, he thought, the same instinct would let her acknowledge her true feelings. Mentally she was stronger than anyone he knew, definitely stronger than he. Would that same mental strength make her hold on to the thought she wasn't cut out for any other life except her work with MRA?

Luke wondered what he would do if she decided that there was no place in her life for him. For the first time in his life he was at a point where thinking things through didn't seem to serve any purpose.

"Rainbow's End died last night," Juan said quietly, a smile hovering at the corners of his mouth as he tested Luke's concentration.

"Umm."

Rachel was saying something to Mojo, who was riding beside her. Incredibly enough, it had been the Indian who had gotten her to start riding. He'd simply saddled Sabrina and brought the mare to the house one afternoon on a leading rein, informing Rachel the horses needed exercise and they were going for a ride.

A surprised Rachel, Theresa had informed Luke later, had looked at the Indian silently for a minute then nodded and said, "Wait a minute while I change into jeans."

Friendship based on respect had taken root immediately between the pair. They rode every day. Mojo talked to Rachel, something he rarely did with anyone else, and she was perfectly at ease with him. Her riding skills were improving and she didn't seem afraid of the horses anymore.

"Two men broke into Stable A last night," Juan said, his grin threatening to split his face.

"Good," Luke said.

He would send for that beautiful handtooled saddle he'd seen in the catalog last week, maybe give it to her at Christmas.

"Luke, shall we do this some other time?" Juan asked patiently.

"What?" Luke spun around.

"Your mind's not on horse feed at the moment," Juan said politely, but the twinkle in his eyes said a lot more. He glanced at the window. "Maybe you should go for a ride, too."

Luke grinned, not in the least embarrassed to have his thoughts guessed so accurately. He had nothing to hide from the man who was like an uncle to him. "I'm sorry, Juan," he said unrepentantly. "You have my full attention now."

Pulling a chair up to the desk he straddled it and tried to shut out thoughts of the child-woman who robbed his nights of sleep.

"Now that Hannah plans on returning Friday, would you like to go to LA with me on Saturday?" Luke asked Rachel on Thursday morning. "It'll give you a chance to get some shopping done. I have some business to take care of, but that shouldn't take too long. We can see a show at night if you like, stay overnight and return in time for Sunday dinner."

Hannah had called last night to say her back was fine now and she would be home Friday morning. Rachel smoothed back Gordon's baby fine hair. Holding one of his hands, she brushed his fingers against her lips, reveling in the downy softness, taking her time about answering Luke.

Ever since their last kiss he'd been like this. Not crowding her in any way, but letting her know he was waiting for her to come around to his way of thinking. What he didn't know was she could be as stubborn as a gold miner's mule and that she had no intention of giving in to her feelings.

"Let me call Dr. Smith and see if I can get an appointment with him Saturday," Rachel said quietly. "I have to fix up details of my next assignment."

Black clouds moved across Luke's brow. "Dr. Kenton hasn't given you an all clear yet," he pointed out.

"I'll have a blood test done at the MRA headquarters," Rachel replied. "There's nothing wrong with me now. I'm eating like a horse, I can walk for miles without tiring, I sleep like a log and am getting as fat as one of Theresa's cows."

The small dairy that supplied the Diamond Bar with milk was Theresa's domain.

Luke wasn't the least bit amused but he didn't argue, and simply said, "Let me know what you decide." The banging of the study door was the only sign of his tension.

Rachel looked at Gordie sitting comfortably astride her hip and her chin wobbled. He'd become so much a part of her it was going to be difficult to let go. Not that she would have it any other way, now. He turned to her for every little thing, as if he sensed her love for him went deeper than a woman's for just any baby.

"It's for the best, you know," she whispered to him. She gently fingered his curls, filing the memory of their silkiness away for when she would be on the other side of the world.

Rachel leafed through the latest issue of *Parents* as she kept an eye on Gordie. The sun room had been converted into his private domain when he'd started crawling. The only things in there were his toys, an enormous beanbag, a couple of soft armchairs and the rocking chair. Watching him haul himself to his feet and look around at her triumphantly, Rachel said, "That's great, Gordie."

Her mind revolved around a remark Theresa had made a little while ago. She'd said something about how much Robbie and Chris had loved each other and then concluded with, "The wisest people are those who grab at love when it comes around."

Was Theresa trying to get something across to her? That life was short, and people who didn't grab at happiness when they could, were fools? Rachel bit her lip. But foolish was also going into a contract as sacred as marriage without being sure of one's ability to deliver.

Gordie had crawled over to his walker and was banging on it. Rachel put him into the red seat. Propelling himself backward across the room at his normal speed, Gordie came to a halt against the large cushions placed at the end of the room to stop him. As always, he looked amazed when something blocked his way.

Rachel frowned down at her hands. Her body clamored for more of the feelings Luke roused in her, for the right to give those feelings rein. The longer she stayed here the less willpower she had. But she mustn't weaken. To grab what she wanted now, and find out later it wasn't enough to last a lifetime would be disastrous for all of them. There had been enough grief on the Diamond Bar to last everyone a long time.

Gordie let out a wail and Rachel got up to turn the walker around, her decision already made.

As soon as Marie came out to watch Gordie, she would call Dr. Smith in LA and insist on being given her new assignment.

# Chapter Nine

Saturday was picture postcard perfect. The sky looked as if a blue sheet had been fitted over it. There wasn't a single cloud in sight. The temperature promised to go up to the seventies and even the usual early morning chill didn't seem quite as cold with the sun shining so brightly.

Luke had mentioned leaving early. Rachel was up by four-thirty, oddly restless. By five she couldn't stay in bed any longer. Hannah found her in the kitchen taking a pan of perfect muffins out of the oven when she came into the kitchen an hour later.

"Good morning!" Her raised eyebrows conveyed her surprise. "You're an early bird today, aren't you? Those muffins look just about perfect."

"I found a cookbook in the drawer and Theresa said you wouldn't mind if I used it." Maybe she should have gone for a walk instead.

"Of course, I don't mind," Hannah said briskly, "and the fact you've made those is going to give me time to finish my list. Are you sure you don't mind doing some shopping for me? Don't worry if you can't get everything. Midweek Betty and I are going into town for the day.'' Hannah looked at the list, then at the table searching for something. ''Oh, dear. I forgot the wool sample.''

''Shall I get it for you?'' Rachel offered, her eyes on her masterpiece. The muffins really were perfect. Now, if only her other attempts were as successful. Yesterday her cheese sauce had had more lumps than an old pillow, and the day before her cake had been trashed.

''Thanks, but I'm not sure where I put it. My memory's getting worse every day.'' Muttering Hannah left the room.

The remark captured Rachel's attention. It was the first she'd heard of anything being wrong with Hannah's memory. The housekeeper was the perfect historian. She could remember things Grandpa Rob had said clearly. Dates, times, even the season. Listening to her talk about the early days on the ranch was better than reading a book.

Turning to the tiled counter, Rachel made herself some tea. Hannah had returned yesterday with a present for her. A mug with her name on it. Touched, Rachel had hugged her and almost started crying.

''Gaga.''

''Good morning, sweetheart.'' She could barely finish the greeting. The navy sweatpants Luke wore rode low on his hips. Impervious to the cold, he hadn't stopped to pull on the top. Water glistened like dewdrops on his chest and his wet hair testified to the fact he'd just gotten out of the shower. The baby's softness against Luke's powerful muscled chest was incredibly provocative. A pulse broke into a gallop in Rachel's throat.

''He's in a hurry for his bottle.'' Luke reached out to the refrigerator.

"Here, let me help." Shrugging off her trance, Rachel reached for a bottle and plugged in the warmer. This close to Luke the scent of soap mingled with a citrusy after-shave was all around her. Rachel shivered under the combined assault.

"Want me to take him while you get ready?"

Luke skimmed her from head to toe and Rachel felt her color rise. Dressed in jeans and sweater for comfort, she wished now she had something more elegant to wear. But fine feathers stuck on a duck didn't change it into a swan.

"Sure," Luke said easily. "It looks like we're going to have a nice day but take your jacket anyway. It will get cool at night."

"Okay."

Hannah came in as Rachel sat at the kitchen table with a diaper clad Gordie, watching him tug at the bottle in his usual hurry. "Let me take him so you can have a muffin while they're still warm. The list was in my pocket all along."

"No thanks, Hannah." Rachel looked down at the navy blue eyes fixed on her face. "I'll eat with you and Luke."

This was one of the few times in the day that Gordie allowed anyone to cuddle him. He was growing so quickly and the fact she wouldn't be here to revel in the changes made her throat tighten. Gordie smiled up at her and she knew at that moment she wouldn't have changed places with anyone in the world. Maybe one day, when she was very old, she would come back and watch the tapes Luke was always recording with his video camera, catch up on what she'd missed.

Hannah paused a minute and looked at the picture they made before turning away with a self-satisfied smile. She'd timed that little incident just right. That man-eating fortune hunter who had visited them last year had done some good after all. Remembering the way the woman had carried on about how the sight of Luke's bare chest turned her on, Hannah had thought of letting Rachel have a glimpse of it. He usually came in like that first thing in the morning.

Theresa had told her things had cooled off considerably since the tree-cutting expedition. It wasn't the way things were meant to be, and Hannah intended to nudge them back on the right track. A little "turning on" seemed to be in order.

By the time Luke returned dressed in tan jeans and a red open-necked shirt, Gordie was on his exercise mat in the sun room with Rachel, his needs temporarily satisfied.

About to sit down at the table, Luke was arrested by Hannah's words. "Never would have thought you were slow. Stubborn, yes. Slow, no."

Luke looked around. He was the only one in the kitchen with her. "I beg your pardon?"

Maybe Hannah was talking to herself.

"You." Turning from the stove Hannah pointed a wooden spoon at him, clearing away all doubt as to whom she was addressing. "Slow. Stubborn. Mulish." Each word was emphasized by a wave of the spoon. "Are you just going to let Rachel leave? I thought you had more sense than that."

Luke's face remained passive. "The decision to stay has to be hers," he said stiffly.

"What's wrong with a little coaxing?" Hannah demanded. "A little of, 'I won't let you leave'?"

"No." Luke's mind was evidently made up. "For a marriage to have a good chance, the decision has to be made by two people, not one."

"Hmph!" She placed the teapot on the table but said nothing more as Rachel came in.

All this modern psychology was so much nonsense. Thank God, Carlos hadn't suffered from any of it. He'd kissed her senseless, looked her straight in the eye and said, "We're getting married in the fall. You're mine."

Hannah decided to give Luke one more week to make his move. If he hadn't cleaned up his act by then, a diet of boiled carrots might help clear his brain.

Breakfast was a quiet meal, each of them busy with their own thoughts.

"You two have a good time and don't worry about anything here," Hannah ordered, as she stood on the veranda to see them off. "Jason's going to sleep in the house tonight. As it's Saturday, Marie and Theresa won't come over, but Angela and I will manage just fine."

Rachel knew that was true and yet the thought of leaving Gordie, even for twenty-four hours created an empty ache inside. The memory of his scrunched up face went with them, and she turned in her seat to wave and catch a last glimpse.

"He'll be fine," Luke said easily. "Don't worry."

But she did. What if he was cutting another tooth. What if Hannah couldn't find the white cow he had become attached to in the past few days. What if—

"Rachel, you've got frown lines on your face," Luke chided gently. "Gordie's going to be fine."

"I know. It's just that . . ." Her voice trailed away.

"I used to feel the same way in the beginning. I'd call home half an hour after I left, to be told it had taken a second after my car disappeared for Gordie to be back to his normal cheery self."

That sounded right. Gordie was too happy a baby to fret for long.

After a moment's pause Luke said, "The drive shouldn't take more than two and a half to three hours. Have a nap if you want to."

Instead of the pickup, Luke was behind the wheel of a white Mercedes. She hadn't seen it before but then she expected the six car garage to the left of the house had more than just the blue pickup in it.

The land changed as they neared Los Angeles. Here mountains were shaved to make way for developments. New and ugly, without the softness of trees to blend them into their natural background, the houses looked like alien invaders, making Rachel fiercely glad she didn't have to live in the city.

Luke dropped her off at MRA headquarters in the heart of downtown, saying he would pick her up at noon. Rachel nodded. Two hours would give her plenty of time to see Dr. Smith, have her blood tests, maybe even her other shots.

She had barely enough time. Dr. Smith insisted on giving her a tour of headquarters, treating her like some sort of visiting dignitary, introducing her to MRA personnel as one of their most valuable field-workers. He showed her the video room and the new training wing, talking all the while about their need for a director for their volunteer education program. Rachel began to feel slightly light-headed. Was there a reason behind the tour? Dr. Smith seemed to be under the impression she'd changed her mind about returning to Bangladesh. She would have to set him straight on that.

"When do you think I can go back to Bangladesh?" They were back in his office seated across from each other. On the table between them rested a tray with two coffee mugs and a plate of cookies.

"Well..." Dr. Smith pulled a file reluctantly toward him. "How does the New Year sound? We have a group going out the end of January."

"I'd like to go earlier, please."

Dr. Smith looked at her over his glasses. The steadiness of her clear gray eyes seemed to bring him to a decision. "Very well. If you insist on returning earlier I can make arrangements for you to leave on the thirty-first."

She would start the New Year as planned—alone.

Ignoring the tremendous band of pressure around her heart, Rachel got to her feet, holding out her hand. "Thank you, Dr. Smith. I'll get my blood test done here today." A glance at the clock over his head showed she was running out of time. "I'm short on time, so I'll have Dr. Kenton give me the required physical and the necessary shots."

"Before I forget," Dr. Smith said, peering at her over the edge of his glasses again, "would you please thank Mr. Summers for his generous donation to MRA?"

"Donation?" It was the first she'd heard of it.

"Yes." Taking off his glasses, he wiped the lenses and replaced them on his nose, beaming at her over the top of them. "He sent us a check for twenty-five thousand dollars."

"I...I...see." Rachel thanked Dr. Smith for his time and said goodbye.

The reminder to ask Dr. Kenton to bill MRA for his services ringing in her ears, Rachel hurried out of the office and to the medical wing.

Luke was waiting for her when she came out of the blue-and-white building. Rachel's heart gave a mighty bound at the sight of his lithe frame easing out from behind the wheel of the Mercedes to open the door for her. Twenty-five thousand dollars! Why had Luke given such a large amount?"

"How did it go?" He didn't make any effort to start the car, though it was in front of a No Parking sign. Rachel's nerve endings quivered with awareness as she faced him. It wasn't such a big car after all, and it seemed to shut out the rest of the world.

"Dr. Smith gave me two options to consider. I need time to think about them. The blood test delayed me. I hope you didn't have to wait long?" Her sentences came out the way she felt. Unsettled, disturbed, *edgy*.

With a shake of his head, Luke negated the fifteen minutes he'd waited. He'd easily picked up the nervous rasp in her voice. "What are the options?"

"One, I stay here and oversee the volunteer training program. Two, I go back to Bangladesh."

"Three, you marry me and live at the Diamond Bar." Smoothly Luke turned the key in the ignition and merged into the downtown lunch-hour traffic.

Stunned, Rachel looked at Luke. He'd tossed the proposal out so casually, as if it was just something to think about, like which clothes to wear for a special occasion.

"I beg your—" Maybe he hadn't said it . . . maybe it was just the traffic whizzing past them in five parallel lanes that had made her imagine the words.

"You heard right." Luke threw her a quick glance. "You have three options, not two."

So much for trying to get a message across, Rachel, thought. Why was he so stubborn? Didn't he know there were much bigger, better fish in the ocean? All ready to jump out to meet him?

The ache within her intensified into a nagging pain at the thought. Being a dog in the manger wasn't easy.

Luke didn't seem to expect an answer right away and Rachel let the silence grow while she mulled over her options. Her heart had chosen instantly but her head wouldn't agree.

Ten minutes later they were out of the traffic, sitting in a small, elegant restaurant. The restaurant was family owned, and everyone knew Luke and came out to ask how Gordie was. Informed she was Chris's cousin, Mama and Papa Patrini's beaming smiles intimated happily-ever-after was in sight after all.

Rachel stole a glance at Luke as he talked to the younger Patrinis, wondering if he was upset by the innuendos. His face gave nothing away. He'd performed his chameleon act again. No one would take them for anything other than good friends who wanted nothing from each other except enjoyable companionship.

"Do you like Italian food?" Luke asked over the top of the menu when they were alone at last. "They offer a few American dishes, as well, if you'd rather have that."

"I don't know much about Italian food." She couldn't remember ever trying any except for spaghetti sauce out of a jar and garlic bread from the grocery store when she was younger. "I'd like to try some, though."

Their tossed salads came with the best garlic bread Rachel had ever tasted, and to follow she had the shrimp fettuccine.

"That was delicious," she told Luke a little while later, staring at her empty plate in surprise.

He grinned and raised a hand to the waiter. "Try some of their gelato. It has quite a reputation."

Rachel nodded weakly, wondering if she would be able to do any shopping after such a large meal.

The ice cream was smooth and had a wonderful flavor. "Mmm. Want to try some?"

Luke hadn't ordered any dessert, just tea. Now he looked up and the little flares in the center of his eyes set quivers leaping in her stomach as he nodded. "Yes."

There was something in the way he watched as she scooped up a teaspoonful and held it out to him that set butterflies dancing in her stomach. Manacling her wrist gently to steady it, he bent to the spoon and closed his mouth around it, his eyes sliding to her lips, their message unmistakable.

"Delicious."

Rachel felt as weak as a newborn foal. Getting through the rest of her ice cream placed a severe strain on her throat muscles.

"Shall we go?" Luke picked up his American Express card, opening a soft brown wallet to slip it inside. "Before I forget, let me give you this."

"This" was a credit card, shiny gold, with her name on it. Rachel stared at it, transfixed. "What's that for?"

"Your shopping spree."

"I have my own money," she said stiffly.

"I know," Luke said easily, "but unless you're carrying it all around with you, you're going to need some other kind of guarantee for cashing your checks."

"I see." She hadn't thought of that. She didn't have a valid driver's license, or even a local address on her checks. That might be a problem in some stores.

"If anyone gives you a hard time about accepting a check, just use the credit card and later you can make out a check to me for the amount you've spent."

He always made everything sound so cut-and-dried. Yet for a simple, straightforward man he was responsible for creating endless confusion within her.

Rachel picked up the shiny slip of plastic. It felt like lead in her hand. "Thank you."

Luke guided her out with his hand on the small of her back. Her body burned where he touched it. Holding herself stiffly, she hoped he wouldn't guess the desire to turn to him was overwhelming her.

As they drove to the Glendale Galleria, he told her about the rooms he'd booked in Pasadena and the show he thought she might enjoy. The hotel he named was one of the best. Rachel wondered if her bank account held enough money to pay for her room.

"We have about four and a half hours here," Luke said as he pulled up in the parking area. "We can come back tomorrow if you don't finish today."

Rachel felt her mouth drop. Four and a half hours? Did Luke think she was buying marble to repair the Taj Mahal. An hour—tops—should get her everything on her list and Hannah's.

Inside the Galleria, Rachel felt her lower jaw drop again. It was like a multistoried Ali Baba's cave. There were people everywhere. Everyone seemed to know exactly where they were going. Two muscled youths with spiky hairdos passed them, looking at her curiously and without being aware of it Rachel moved closer to Luke.

Luke's splayed his fingers and linked them with hers. Immediately Rachel knew he had no intention of leaving her alone. Tugging her gently forward he said, "Let's start right here."

He left her in the Misses section of the large department store, saying he would be back in a while. Rachel looked around, her head whirling at the selection around her. Walking around, she just looked at all the racks for a while, now and then touching something.

Luke returned with a packet to find her still looking. "If you don't like anything here we can always go into the mall. There are dozens of other shops to choose from."

"It's not that," Rachel said quickly. "It's just that there's so much to choose from I don't know where to start."

She looked like a child in a toy shop and Luke laughed. "Take your time. I'm going to the hardware section to look for a couple of things."

Rachel finally chose a silky red dress with a gray sequined flower on one shoulder, a slip to go with it and an emerald green velour jogging suit. There really wasn't any point in buying more. By this time next month she would be back in Bangladesh and have no use for these clothes. But at least for the time being she wanted to do Luke and Gordie proud. Hannah had said they had lots of visitors dropping by Christmas week. Rachel didn't want any of them to think she was a poor relation.

Selecting warm velour robes for Hannah and Theresa, both of whom had complimented her on hers, a pair of large, flashy earrings for Angela and a handbag for Marie didn't take too long. In the children's section she picked out some clothes for Gordie. There was something deeply satisfying about shopping for the baby. The thought that even when she wasn't there he would use the outfits she'd gotten him was a nice one. She was paying for her purchases when Luke returned. He looked at the pile of clothes on the counter but didn't comment.

"Where to next?" he asked, relieving her of her shopping bag.

"A bookshop and then a craft store."

They strolled the length of the mall. Luke's hand around her shoulders steered her through the crowd, kept her safe from being jostled. The contact sparked off so much heat Rachel almost expected to see smoke coming out of her ears.

A few minutes later, Rachel stopped in front of a shoe store. On the pretext of looking at a pair of high-heeled sandals with delicate straps, she moved away from Luke. Any more of those tantalizing brushes against him and she would self-combust.

"Want to go in and try them on?" Luke asked.

Rachel shook her head. None of those ultrafeminine, dainty shoes would be any good where she was going and the black heels she'd bought the first day would do with her red dress.

At the bookstore she purchased a book on hummingbirds for Juan and a light paperback cookbook for herself. After finding the macramé book and the latest historical romances on Hannah's list, Rachel picked up four cloth books for Gordie. She'd found a *National Geographic* with pictures of animals and showed it to him one day, and he'd astounded them all by pointing to it the next day and jumping up and down: his way of asking for something. With the exception of Luke, her gift list was complete. She had ordered a video game for David, an elegant pen for Jason and a canteen for Mojo out of a catalog. Maybe Jason would take her to Santa Barbara with him one day and she would find something there for Luke.

The craft store didn't take long. A helpful assistant took Hannah's list and the samples and found everything in record time, while Rachel looked at the intricate cross-stitch designs on the wall, wishing she had the talent and patience to do things like that.

"That's the last of my shopping," she announced as she was handed her package.

"Are you sure? Luke seemed taken aback.

Rachel nodded. "Yes, but you go ahead and get the rest of your things."

They walked to another store and Luke said, "Let's go in here for a minute. I need a couple more gifts."

Rachel wandered over to the women's section. She could tell this store was different. The plushy carpet, the quiet elegance, the saleswomen who looked like models. Her first check of a price tag made her think she would be paying for the rarefied atmosphere if she bought anything in the store, but a look at the quality of the merchandise and Rachel knew it would be worth every penny she spent.

"May I help you with anything today?"

Rachel looked at the woman her own age dripping with sophistication and stammered, "N...no thank you. I'm just looking."

Rachel wandered over to the cosmetics counter and looked at the display in the glass case. She wouldn't know what to do with a tenth of these things.

"We're doing makeovers today. Would you like one?"

She looked up at the older, perfectly made-up woman across the counter and then glanced doubtfully down at the cosmetics on display.

"It's free. You don't need to buy anything," the woman coaxed.

About to shake her head Rachel stopped. Why not? There wasn't any harm in knowing the right way to do her face, even if where she was going she was lucky if she had the time to wash it twice a day.

"All right."

The woman introduced herself as Helen and talked non-stop as she went through her routine. "You have an excellent complexion. It's just a little dry. Be sure and use plenty of moisturizer. Do you use foundation? Well, I'm not going to, either. A dab of powder will do. Now, a little blush just so. Do you see how that highlights your cheekbones? What excellent bone structure. All you need is a tinge of color. I'm going to use a little more makeup on your eyes. They're so beautiful. What's your favorite color in clothes?"

"Red." Since when? a tiny voice mocked. Since Luke's eyes took on a glow everytime he looked at her in her red sweater?

As Helen did her eyes, saying something about enhancing them, part of Rachel's mind wandered away to the summer she'd spent with Christina. The cousins had experimented every day with makeup and different hairstyles.

Aunt Mary had bought her a few basic items as a gift. When she'd returned home her father had thrown everything away and told her she wasn't to do herself up like a cheap tart while she lived under his roof. He'd put up with enough of that from her mother.

It hadn't even hurt. Rachel had just retreated to the spot in her mind that had stored up every single moment of her wonderful summer. It was the one place her father couldn't follow.

"There. That shade is perfect for you." With a start Rachel realized the huge, luminous eyes staring back at her from the mirror on the counter were hers. Helen had used a soft coral on her lips. Color made them seem fuller, gave them a pout. "Here's some tissue. Blot your lips and then I'm going to go over them once more. I'm all done now. You look lovely." Standing back, Helen looked at her, a satisfied smile on her face. "Wish I could get this effect on all my clients. All I used was powder, blush, an eye pencil, some shadow and lipstick. You look like a million dollars. Don't you think so, sir?"

Rachel almost fell off the stool. In the back of her mind she'd entertained the thought of washing her face before she saw Luke. It was too late now. Raising her chin, she faced him.

Luke stood three feet away, his glance raking her face. Slowly her gaze swiveled away from him to the mirror in front of her. Nervousness snaked up her spine. It was as if Helen had ripped her cover to shreds and revealed Rachel's true identity...the face that stared back was a woman's. Wanting, desiring, *needing*.

"Let me see." Ignoring the makeup consultant, Luke put a finger under her chin, raising her face. He could tell Rae was doing her high wire routine again. The apprehension she tried to mask was at the forefront of her eyes.

"I was just going to wash my face."

His eyes narrowed. *This* was what her fear was all about? That he might disapprove of her decision to have her face done? He bit back an expletive. The fact that he didn't think she needed cosmetics to improve her looks didn't matter. What mattered was that he had to convince her she had a right to spread her wings without being afraid.

"Very nice." Deliberately he let his eyes skim her face again, making sure his voice was warm, bordering on wolf-ish. He skimmed his thumb along the edge of her bottom lip and saw the delicate color return to her face. "You should use that color on your lips more often."

Rachel looked at him. The intensity of his gaze as their eyes met was almost like an electric shock. Luke dismissed the blaze of gratitude he saw in Rachel's eyes. It wasn't what he wanted from her.

"How much does all the stuff you've used cost?" Luke asked Helen over his shoulder. Buying it would let Rae know she could experiment to her heart's content.

Rachel saw Helen's eyes widen before she quickly punched numbers into the cash register terminal and said hopefully. "A hundred and twenty-five dollars, thirty-two cents.

"We'll take it."

Stunned by Luke's reaction, Rachel couldn't think of a thing to say. He'd looked at her as if... as if she was good enough to eat.

Luke looked at her again, brushed a strand of hair off her forehead. "Chris told me once there's an excellent beauty salon here. Do you want to get your hair styled?"

The makeup consultant opened her mouth to protest but Luke silenced her with a look. He couldn't bear the thought himself that Rae might want to cut it, or have it styled in one of those frizzy, modern creations that reminded him of a bramble bush. He loved the way she was wearing it today. The loose knot with its escaping curls was the perfect frame for her cameolike features.

Love didn't enforce though. Love understood and gave the other person room to grow, to change.

"I don't think so, thanks."

Rachel got off her stool and stood quietly by as Luke paid for all the makeup. She would write him a check for it later, explain that if she'd wanted the cosmetics she would have bought them herself. There was no point in making a scene here.

"Anything else you'd like to get?"

"No, thanks." Rachel shook her head and thanked Helen, who hadn't stopped smiling.

"You have a nice day and a wonderful holiday," the older woman said warmly.

"Would you like to go up to the next level and look around?"

Rachel hesitated and Luke said quickly, "You'd rather leave."

She nodded. "I've had my fill of looking." She was more tired than she was after a few hours spent chasing Gordie. That was a pleasurable tiredness, this was just a weariness of spirit she couldn't explain. Impatience to be out of the mall surged up in her, mingled with the longing to go straight back to the Diamond Bar, but she forced herself to be polite. "But what about your shopping?" Luke only had a couple of small packages of his own.

"I have everything I need. Let's go."

They were at the hotel in fifteen minutes. Their rooms were on the third floor, across from each other.

"Shall we meet about six for dinner?" Luke opened the door to her room and stood aside.

Rachel took in the opulent interior. This place must have cost the earth.

"Six is fine," she said absently, wondering how she was going to repay him. Another blank check? She only hoped her bank account held enough.

He set her packages down on a handy chair. She'd suggested leaving all but one in the car, but Luke had carried everything upstairs, saying she might like to look over her purchases and decide if there was anything else she needed.

"See you in a little while then."

Rachel explored her room and the adjoining bathroom curiously. It was all very elegant. Like a child she looked at the room service menu and opened the drawers of the desk, picking up the fine writing paper and examining the texture.

Looking up, she caught her reflection in the mirror. The strangeness of her own face startled her for a second, then she leaned closer, peering at her reflection. Assuming a model's hauteur, she struck a pose.

Truth elbowed its way in. It wasn't any use. No makeover would change the way she was inside.

Turning away, Rachel strolled to the window.

As far as the eyes could see there were buildings and more buildings, hemming her in and making her face the truth. Resting her head against the window, Rachel thought of the evening ahead.

The tap on his door surprised Luke. Wiping the lather from his face with the towel draped around his neck he went to the door. He hadn't ordered anything from room service.

"Rae. Is something wrong?" The sight of her through the peephole had startled him. The fact she had her arms wrapped around herself the way she had in court was definitely cause for alarm. "What is it?" Drawing her into the room Luke shut the door. "Aren't you feeling well?" He put a hand up to her forehead.

Rachel moved back and shook her head. He saw the movement of her throat as she swallowed hard. Whatever it was, was costing her. Gently he brushed the hair back from her forehead. "What is it?" he asked again.

"I . . . I know this is going to sound very silly but I want to ask you something."

"Sure."

Her tongue stole out to moisten her lips and she half turned away from him before she spoke. "Can we go back to the Diamond Bar?"

"Now?"

"Now." Her head was down. "I know I'm being an awful nuisance and I can't explain the way I feel but I want to go—"

She stopped herself before the last word but Luke knew it was *home*. His muscles tightened with the longing to sweep her into his arms and tell her that that was what he wanted as well. All he said was, "Give me five minutes."

"I'm sorry if I spoilt your one evening of relaxation," Rachel said hurriedly. "I'll write you a check for the cost of the hotel rooms."

He must think her an immature spoiled brat. What kind of woman wouldn't like to be wined and dined in style? No culture. That had to be it. She was sure the women in Luke's world reveled in this sort of thing.

"I used to do this all the time. I don't crave this kind of entertainment anymore." He made short work of the apology. "I just thought it would give you a chance to relax after being cooped up with Gordie all week . . . that *you* might enjoy an evening on the town."

He'd done it for her? His honesty had to be matched. "This is what makes me feel cooped up." He knew she meant the so-called civilized trappings. She touched a hand to her face, indicating the layers of cosmetics. "I feel as if I have to force myself to play a part I don't want to, be someone else and I can't do it."

The hand that brought her chin up was firm and warm. The eyes that met hers blazed with something she couldn't define. "Don't apologize for being yourself, Rae. Very few people have the courage to do that. The urge to run with the pack, the need to do the 'in' things, to be accepted, makes most people strangers to themselves. It took me a very long while to realize the only person I owed anything to was myself."

She stood there, aching for the touch of Luke's mouth. By his stance she sensed a waiting in him, as well. If she made one move toward him . . . her gaze flickered to the bed, then away.

Rachel found herself facing the door before she even felt his hands on her shoulders. Luke's voice was soft by her ear. "The last one packed and ready has to do the dishes for a week."

By the time he got on the freeway the sun had set. Winter darkness, soft as the color of her eyes when she looked at Gordie, surrounded them.

Luke's hands tightened on the wheel as he thought of the way she'd summoned her courage to come to him. He fought the urge to yell at her that he was just another human being . . . as frightened of her reactions as she was of his. But it was a reaching out . . . progress. He would have to be patient to win it all.

There was so much he could offer her but none of it . . . not even his love would be any use if Rachel didn't find herself first, and realize what it was that she wanted out of life. He'd heard of people swept off their feet into marriage, who woke up later to discover they hadn't had time to think about what they were in, or even if this was what they wanted out of life. A mistake like that would cost more than expending a little patience now.

She didn't know it but he'd called Waylon Smith from his room and been informed of her decision to return to Bangladesh already. Rehabilitation in the flood devastated areas, he'd been told, would keep her in that country for close to two years and then she would be transferred to another area.

He was taking an awfully big risk with all this waiting. For a man who didn't believe in gambling, to leave the rest of his life to chance was very hard, but there was no viable alternative to letting her make her own choices.

Switching on the overhead light, Luke looked at Rae and a smile softened his mouth. They had come a long way since that day in court and she'd definitely benefited by her stay on the ranch.

So had Gordie. He loved the way she carried him on her hip. Sometimes she held him monkey fashion to her chest as if she couldn't get enough of him. At others, she sat cross-legged with him on the floor, talking to him, reading to him. Luke knew Gordie sensed exactly how she felt about him. He'd begun to look for her now, and yesterday when they had both held out their arms to him he'd chosen to go to Rae.

It wasn't only Gordie. Hannah and Theresa were always singing her praises. Juan and Jason couldn't do enough for her. Mojo brought her wildflowers and took her riding. The Indian had cut his hair, came to work clean shaven these days and kept out of trouble.

There was so much for her here, but only Rachel could reach out for it. No one else could help her with this one decision.

Looking at her once more, he switched off the light.

She was like a flame. Small but steady. Holding her own against all odds. Giving everything, asking nothing. Her essential goodness provided the fuel that kept the flame burning. Luke wondered if ever a time would come when she would let him cup that flame. Not to diminish its splendor in any way, just to protect it, so it could burn more brightly.

The slamming of the car door woke Rachel.

"Everything's fine," Luke was saying and Rachel could make out Hannah's outline in the doorway. "We just wanted to come home." Through sleep-riddled eyes she saw Jason come out, say goodnight, and veer off toward the garages whistling.

"If everything's fine, I'm going back to bed." Hannah swept away, before Rachel could get out of the car.

After a wash she slipped along the corridor to Gordie's room. The impulse to lift him and hold him close was almost too much to resist. He looked like a little angel. Exquisite, peaceful, precious. If only she could make time stand still, keep Gordie at this baby stage a little longer, stay with him a few more days. Rachel wasn't aware of the big sigh that escaped her.

"Let's go into the kitchen," Luke urged, close to Rachel's ear and she jumped. He trailed one strong finger down Gordie's cheek before he followed her out.

They raided the refrigerator, piling the coffee table in the family room with their bounty. Cream of broccoli soup, cold chicken, crusty bread, half a bowl of trifle. Food had never tasted so good. They talked in whispers, not wanting to disturb Hannah.

As Luke carried their dishes to the sink, Rachel gave in to an impulse. Crossing to the elaborate music system against the wall, she pressed a button and turned the dial till she found the right station. Dreamy music floated into the air.

Sensing Luke come up behind her she turned into his arms. She couldn't see his face, so she didn't know if he was surprised. He held her close, wrapping her in his warmth. The night receded as she lay her head on his shoulder.

They danced well together, not changing their pace when the music switched to something fast and upbeat. He bent a little, rested his cheek against hers, the smoothness of his face reminding Rachel he'd been shaving when she had knocked on the door of his room. She inhaled the splash of his after-shave, then burrowed her head in his shirtfront, wanting more of Luke's own scent.

She thought of the day, how wonderful it was to be in Luke's company, his reaction to the makeover. She held her eyes wide-open. If she blinked now the tears would fall, and it would be difficult explaining to Luke that she was crying because he was the nicest man she knew.

Luke turned his lips into her hair. Content to be ensconced in the warmth of his arms, Rachel drifted on dreamily, aware they were creating moments she would never forget. The moon, as if aware of the magnitude of the moment, sailed majestically out from behind some clouds.

It was a lover's moon, Rachel thought dreamily.

Electrified by the unbidden scenes romping in her imagination, she realized she was picking up momentum like an avalanche. If she didn't stop now, she would never be able to. And there was always a morning after. Reaching rock bottom would mean being smashed to smithereens.

Stepping away from Luke she looked up at him and infused casualness into her voice. "I'll always remember this."

Luke stiffened. There it was again. The warning. Firm, direct, unchanging. Letting him know she'd made her plans.

That she was going to get on with them, no matter what. His shoulders bunched as tension crept up his spinal cord.

"Have you made a decision?"

He could sense rather than see her nod. "I'm booked on a flight out of LAX on the thirty-first."

Pain splintered in his chest, as the last sliver of hope fled. "I see."

Their feet had stopped moving. They faced each other like boxers in a ring. The closeness of a few minutes ago might never have been.

Rachel waited a while. When she realized Luke wasn't going to say anything she whispered, "I think I'll turn in now. Thank you for everything."

As she slipped away, Luke turned and strode into the darkness.

## Chapter Ten

Gordie sat at the breakfast table, his face smeared with oatmeal, when Rachel entered the kitchen the next morning. She'd started him feeding himself and he seemed to enjoy it.

"Good morning."

Aware of Luke leaning against the counter, mug in hand, she bent down and searched for a spot on Gordie's face that wasn't buried under oatmeal to plop her kiss on. He held his spoon out to her, generously offering her a taste of the cereal.

"No thanks." Rachel laughed, dodging the wavering, dripping, spoon. "I'll get my own."

Taking bowls out of the cabinet, she set the table in the eating nook in the kitchen.

Luke's silence after the brief good morning weighed heavily in the air. She'd barely slept. Knowing what was for the best and doing it were two entirely different things. Rachel had tossed and turned, beset with uncertainties about going away, more terrified of staying on. Her cogitating mind repeatedly came up with and discarded alternate plans of action.

She picked up the table mats and put them down. The sunshine gave her something to talk about.

"Nice day, isn't it?" Anything was better than this silence.

Luke shrugged. "It's cold and windy outside."

End of a great conversation. She aimlessly opened a drawer and shut it.

The clatter as the bowl fell made her jump. Rachel turned to Gordie in time to see his face crumple. Leaning over in his high chair he looked at the upended bowl of cereal on the floor. His face scrunched up, a sure sign tears weren't far away. The noise had obviously startled him. Before either of them could say a word, he looked up and held his hands out to Rachel, "Mama!"

Rachel stood rooted to the spot. Mama! Her brain absorbed the word, vibrated with the echoes. He must have picked up the word from David and Angela. They called Theresa that. But why apply it to her?

*Oh, Gordie,* she thought, *not you, too.*

Dimly she heard Luke say, "That's all right, Gordie." Loud wails split the air. Picking him up he patted his nephew's back and shushed him. "Sit down, Rae."

She looked from Gordie's face to Luke's for the first time that morning. His gaze rested on her like the lash of silk—warm and understanding. Suddenly it was all too much. She turned and ran out of the house.

"Good morning."

Luke turned to see Theresa entering the kitchen. Putting Gordie back in his high chair he said, "Give him some more cereal will you please, Theresa?"

"Certainly."

Luke knew where he would find her. His feet carried him to the little glade. It had been his mother's favorite spot, as well.

She was lying facedown on the cold ground, weeping as if her heart were breaking. Poor little doe. He'd seen the expression on her face when Gordie had sprung his surprise. The gamut of emotions warring there had confirmed what he suspected. She was terrified that the stone fortress she'd constructed around her emotions was disintegrating.

He lifted her effortlessly, settled her so her head rested against his shoulder and simply held her. It took a while for her crying to dwindle to great big sobs that racked her body from time to time.

It all bubbled over as he soothed her. "I'm...not any good...at loving. I...didn't want G...Gordie to get attached to me. I...never meant to hurt anyone."

"You haven't," he whispered, rubbing her back gently. "Love isn't something that can be doled out on request. It's either there or it isn't."

"I don't want Gordie to be hurt when I leave."

"Then stay."

"I can't. Don't you see that? I'm not like Chris. I'm not any good at personal relations."

A cannonball of anger formed low in Luke's stomach. What kind of human monster had made her feel like this?

"What makes you think so?"

"My mother couldn't stand me. That's why she left us. My father had no time for me after she went away. I tried so hard to get him to like me but he...he never cared. He said it was all because of me."

Luke's face set in harsh lines. "Your father didn't know what he was talking about, Rachel," he said sternly. "He was blaming you for his own inadequacies."

He could tell she was calming down from the way her breathing evened out and he continued, absently caressing her head. "Everyone here thinks you're wonderful. Hannah says you're the answer to her prayers. Juan and Theresa sing your praises all the time. David says you're cool, even though you haven't found the right recipe for chocolate chip cookies yet. Jason can't take his eyes off you and Mojo works late just to have the time to go riding with you. Dr. Smith tells me Tom Atwell can't stop praising you, either. He showed me your file. One remark of Dr. Atwell's on a report stuck in my mind. He said you were a wonderful, caring human being with an endless capacity for giving. All these people can't be wrong, Rae."

After a while, she raised a red, blotchy face to his and sniffed. "You talked to Dr. Smith about me?"

Luke nodded and gently brushed a wisp of hair off her warm forehead. He trailed his fingers down the side of her face, aching with the restraint he'd placed on himself. She was at her most vulnerable now. To comfort her in the way he wanted to would be selfish. "Yes. When I called him to tell him you weren't well."

Luke held her lightly, turning his head so his lips rested against her temple. "I love you, Rae."

The words tipped into a pool of silence. The widening circles of stillness told Luke it would take more than words to coax her out of the dark woods of self-torture once and for all.

In the distance a horse whinnied. The bit of sky he could glimpse was framed with evergreens and cloudless. Luke thought back to the filly Rob had bought last year. Ill-treated by her previous owner, Golden Girl was in an awful condition when she'd arrived at the Diamond Bar. She wouldn't let anyone near her.

Rob had won her over not by chasing her, or coaxing her with tidbits but just by going into her paddock daily and standing there, talking to her in a monotone, and waiting. She'd come to him in a week.

Rachel needed time and patience. He was man enough to give her both, no matter what it cost him.

"I didn't mean to get your shirt wet." Her fingertips on his shirtfront heated his body to fire, threatening to incinerate his recent resolutions.

"It doesn't matter. Feeling better?"

This time he let her pull away, sit up. It was safer for both of them.

"Yes. Thank you."

Her back was to him and he could sense her panic as she searched for her familiar barricade. It must have been difficult when she found nothing there.

"Don't worry too much, Rae. Things have a way of sorting themselves out."

There was no answer. He didn't expect one. Standing up he held a hand out to her. She took it, standing within an inch of him. His glance slid from her eyes to her lips. Slightly swollen from her bout of tears, they didn't help his willpower. For a moment he was tempted to thrust logic aside and make love to her. But with her he knew if he wanted it all, passion alone would never work. For the success of their future, Rae's mind had to acknowledge and accept her feelings.

Swallowing hard, Luke flung an arm around her shoulders and tucked her into his side. "Let's go home."

*Mama.* At odd moments during the day Rachel found herself saying the word under her breath. What a wonderful word. If only, she thought closing her eyes to shut out the piercing sweetness of hope, if only she could really claim the title. Gordie's mama. Luke's wife. She knew a date in January had been set for his official adoption of Gordie. By then she would be on the other side of the world. Back where she felt safe. Where nothing or no one would ever again touch her heart.

This time, Rachel knew, she would never return.

In the days that followed, she wrapped her presents, helped Hannah with some extra baking and spent all her spare time with Gordie. She called Dr. Kenton's office and went down to Santa Barbara with Jason on Friday for her shots. Afterward Rachel opened a new bank account and transferred all her money into it. She would leave the savings book on Luke's table. Explanations were redundant.

Luke came out of his office at night to find only two places set at the kitchen table. Raising an eyebrow he looked at Hannah. Was Bud picking her up for another shopping spree?

Hannah banged a dish of boiled carrots on the table, serving him a much too generous helping. "Rachel doesn't want any dinner. She's running a fever."

Luke's brows snapped together. "Why didn't you tell me earlier?"

"I didn't know till half an hour ago." The clipped words warned he was in for a lifetime of boiled carrots. Served at breakfast, lunch and dinner. "Thought she was wrapping presents in her room but found her in bed with a temperature of a hundred and two."

He was out of the room before she'd finished talking. With a cursory tap on the door, he entered Rachel's room. She was propped up in bed, looking very tired.

"What's wrong, Rae?" The sight of her flushed face knotted his stomach and the hand he put against her cheek trembled slightly.

"It's nothing." Her eyes, fever bright, held a shot of some other emotion as she looked at him. "I always have this reaction to the typhoid shot."

"Ty—" It took a whole moment to get air back into his lungs. So, she was going ahead with her plans. Their talk hadn't changed a thing. "When did you have the shot?"

"This afternoon. Jason was going in for supplies and he gave me a ride to Dr. Kenton's."

"I see." Jason would do well to consult his astrologer about his future.

He looked at Rachel and his anger vanished. Her saucer-like eyes and her arms wrapped around her body sent their own message. Stubborn little thing. Their talk in the grove might never have been.

"Why do you have the pillow under your arm?"

"The cholera shot. My arm always swells a bit," she said apologetically.

Damn. How many needles had they stuck in her?

"Let me see." The gentleness of his hands as he looked at the pearlike swelling on her arm was at odds with the set of his mouth. His fingers traced the area lightly, sending tremors of delight through her body. "How many shots did you have?"

"Only two. Next week I go back for the hepatitis shot, and then I'm all set."

"I see." He leaned forward to check her forehead but it was cold and slightly clammy. She must have taken something for the fever.

He swung away, jammed both hands into his pockets and stared out the window.

"Luke?"

Rachel's heart was going like a trip-hammer. It would be better if he shouted, said something. The silence was like a slap.

He turned to face her. "So, you've decided to leave on the thirty-first as planned?"

"It's what I have to do."

Anger surged against the dam of self-control. Fear he'd lost her flicked a switch that lifted the gates, and words raged through. "I would never have taken you for a coward, Rae, but that's what you are, aren't you? You aren't going to face the truth till it's too late. Maybe you never will. When are you going to realize that life doesn't come with any guarantees? If it did, Chris and Rob would still be here today, there would be no pain, no suffering, no hunger in the entire world."

Anger drained out and a searing pain took its place. The pain of losing her. The pain of an empty future. Crossing over to the bed, he sat on the edge and placed a hand on either side of Rachel's head, not touching her. He pinned her gaze with his own. "Life only gives us opportunities, Rae. It's up to us to make things work. When you were a child, you couldn't do much about what happened to you." Almost of its own volition, one hand came up and brushed the wisps of hair off her forehead. "But now you're an adult. You have the power to change things. Are you ever going to stop running long enough to give yourself a chance to use that power?"

The door closing behind Luke was like a curtain coming down. The play was over.

Only no one applauded.

## Chapter Eleven

Christmas was a blur of visitors, Hannah's special dinner, concentrating on keeping her mind and eyes off Luke.

Rachel had never received so many presents in her entire life. The fact that the people who gave them to her wrapped genuine affection with their gifts touched her deeply.

Luke handed her a slim box from under the tree Christmas morning, saying, "From Gordie and me. Wear it in good health." The Gucci watch with the single diamond had robbed her of speech. He'd thanked her for the picture of Gordie in the silver frame, leaving the room before she could respond.

He'd slipped back into the role of perfect host. Polite, cool, remote.

While there were people around it had been easy to avoid him, but the day after Christmas Rachel wondered how she would get through the next few days. Her emotions were like tightly stretched violin strings . . . the tiniest increase of tension would be disastrous.

Deliberately, she went into the kitchen late that morning to avoid the possibility of running into a bare-chested Luke again.

Piling the clothes she would be taking with her on the kitchen table, Rachel checked them against her list. Ordering them through a catalog had saved time and energy. She had everything she needed.

Hannah's stiff back reminded her of the change in their roles. The housekeeper had grown increasingly quiet over the past few days, and it was Rachel who filled the silences with words these days.

"I have to wash these things before I can pack. Otherwise the starchiness is terrible in the heat," she was saying when Luke entered the kitchen.

His features froze as he took in the pile of white clothes. Silently he crossed over to the stove for a cup of tea. Hannah took the towel on her shoulder and swiped viciously at an imaginary speck on the counter.

Luke filled his cup, turned to rest against the counter. "I've got some business in Sacramento that I've been putting off for a while." His gaze rested on a spot on the window as he spoke to the room at large. "I can't do that any longer. Think I might have to leave tomorrow."

"How long will you be away?" Hannah didn't seem the least bit surprised at the news.

Rachel snipped at the price tags on her clothes, head bowed, waited for Luke's answer, heart in mouth.

"I'll be back late New Year's eve." *After she had left.* "Do you think Betty and Bud would like to come up for a visit till after New Year?"

"They'd be delighted," Hannah said without an ounce of pleasure in her own voice.

"Great. I'll make the arrangements then." He was gone, leaving behind a silence that pressed down heavily on Rachel. Picking up her clothes, she took them into the large laundry room and flung them into the washer.

It was best this way, she told herself fiercely, as she angrily swiped at the treacherous tears. Luke had taken matters into his own hand, accepted her stubbornness and decided to leave the field clear for her departure. He was making it easy for both of them.

The relief she ought to feel was conspicuous by its absence.

She was in the family room trying to concentrate on Agatha Christie's, *Death on the Nile*, late that evening when she heard the study door open and shut.

"I'm leaving at four in the morning, so I'll wish you goodbye now."

She stood on feet that didn't seem to be there. She kept her tone steady. "Goodbye, Luke. Thanks for everything."

She stared at the second button of his shirt.

"Sure." He could have been talking to anyone. "Keep in touch. We'd like to know how you're getting on." She might have been going to LA, instead of halfway around the world. "I'll send you pictures of Gordie so you can keep track of how he grows."

He held his hand out, shook hers briefly, dropped it and put a hand on her shoulder.

This is it, Rachel thought, this is the last kiss. A minute later she was standing alone. All she'd felt was a friendly squeeze of her shoulder as if Luke were some old uncle wishing her farewell.

* * *

The day of her departure dawned clear and bright. Rachel woke oddly grumpy. Her eyes looked back at her from the bathroom mirror, ringed with dark circles. "If this," she told herself waspishly, "is what getting your own way does to you, I hope you don't get it too often."

Making a face at her reflection she reached for a washcloth. She would shower just before she left.

She'd taken over the morning hour with Gordie since Luke's departure. He was doing well with a feeding cup, but still liked his bottle first thing in the morning and last thing at night.

"I love you, Gordie." She rested her cheek against the soft chubbiness of his and willed her message imprinted in his subconscious. "I always will." He grabbed the first button of her shirt and tried to prise it off.

"Good morning." The brusque tone and the abrupt way Hannah turned to the stove didn't fool Rachel. The housekeeper was hurting as much as she was.

"Hi!" The cheerful façade had to be kept up for a few more hours. "Can I help with breakfast?"

"No." Hannah opened cupboards, slammed them shut, looking for things she already had on the counter. "Betty and Bud left early this morning for Hearst castle. Asked me to say goodbye for them."

Rachel eyed the stiff back but didn't say anything. She was hanging on to her self-control by a thread. It wouldn't stand the strain of too many words. Even with Betty and Bud there, the last few days hadn't been easy. Yesterday Jason had driven her down to the farm for one last look around. The people who knew her had come up to wish her well, and the more Rachel kept telling everyone she had to go back, the less convinced she herself became of it.

"Breakfast will be ready soon," Hannah said gruffly over her shoulder.

"I'll get Gordie dressed then."

In his room Rachel played peek-a-boo with Gordie and read to him. When Hannah called up the stairs that breakfast was ready, she picked Gordie up and went downstairs, holding him close to her, breathing deeply of his baby smell, storing the feel of him for when she would be alone.

Rachel's favorite blueberry muffins were on the table. At the sight of them her composure almost gave way. She managed one by washing it down with large gulps of water. As soon as Theresa arrived, Rachel excused herself from the table and carried her plate and glass to the sink.

Plucking her jacket off the hook by the side door, she let herself out without saying a word to anyone. The cold air was a challenge she welcomed as she walked briskly up the hill. The grass held traces of morning dew that wet the bottom of her jeans but she didn't notice it. When she reached her favorite spot, Rachel sank on the ground, her back against the log. A quick check of her watch showed it was only ten. She had two hours left before Jason arrived to drive her to Los Angeles. Juan had informed her yesterday of the arrangements Luke had made for her departure.

Luke. Rachel plucked a blade of grass. He'd called every day and talked to Hannah at length. The telephone was held to Gordie's ear, as well, so he could hear Luke's voice. He hadn't asked to speak to her.

Hannah always said "Luke says hello" at the end of the call, but Rachel really wasn't sure if the housekeeper made that up just to be polite.

"Rachel."

She spun to her feet startled. Mojo stood before her. She hadn't heard him come up.

"Mojo. How are you?" She would miss him. There was something about the feelings he harbored that she understood without it being put into words.

"Are you all set to leave?"

"Yes." Rachel turned away so he wouldn't see the pain in her eyes.

"Sabrina's going to miss you."

Rachel swallowed hard. Each link she severed caused a part of her heart to crumble. The milk-white mare was very special.

"This is for you."

She turned and took the crumpled ball of tissue he held out to her. Inside was a delicate necklace in pure silver, turquoise chips enhancing its beauty.

"Thank you." She couldn't protest what it had cost him. Mojo wasn't giving her a gift. He was giving her a bit of himself.

Rachel turned away as the tears poured down her face. By leaving she was robbing Mojo of a friend he needed badly. Those who knew loneliness returned to it when things went wrong.

"Do you remember the first day, when you talked to me?" The measured tones held no emotion.

"Yes." Rachel swiped at her tears with the back of her hand. If talking about it helped him, she wouldn't grudge Mojo the raw ache of relived memories.

"You said I was a coward."

"Only to make you go to the doctor."

"You're the real coward, aren't you?"

Turning, Rachel faced him. "What do you mean?" She'd told him she had to go back. How much more had he guessed?

"I was afraid the medicine would kill me." His eyes reflected sadness more than anger. And the truth. "You're afraid of trusting your feelings."

He was gone before she could ask him when he'd gotten a degree in psychology.

Everything faded before truth. Excuses, explanations, justifications. Sitting down on the log, Rachel picked up a pine needle and twirled it.

She thought back to the first day in court, the great tension that had been part of her. When Luke had brought her here she had been a bundle of nerves, incapable of functioning on a personal level. She'd come a long way since that day.

Her insecurities had been bandaged in acceptance, her self esteem raised sky high. Love had eased her pain, cleared the mists of confusion that surrounded her past. She'd been given time to think, time to search herself for the truth about the past.

Bit by bit she'd remembered scenes with her mother in the last week. They had floated to her out of the dim, distant past, free to reach her now that the barrier erected by her childish trauma was no more. Laughing with her, listening to the sound of the ocean in a seashell, having her hair brushed, being tucked into bed with a good-night kiss. One fact had emerged crystal clear. Her mother had loved her. Whatever had driven her away had nothing to do with that love. Rachel knew she would never again torture herself with the thought that she'd caused her parent's breakup.

Luke had given her that.

Looking back now, she couldn't remember a time when she hadn't loved Luke, but the day of the picnic when he'd kissed her awake, she had been sure. Her capacity for loving had never been in any doubt.

Luke had told her she would have to stop running one day. Mojo's words had stopped her long enough to take one long look at the truth. She wanted to face it now, here, re-live every incident and then bury it all here in the spot where she was sure a part of her would always remain.

She had hope. Deep inside her Rachel knew she'd never been short of that precious commodity. Till her father died she had hoped for some sign that he cared for her. It had been hope that had made her take Luke to court. The hope that she would have someone of her own to love. Someone who would love her back.

Love had come to her unexpectedly, not only from the child, but from the man, as well. And she'd refused it.

Rachel wondered if emotional cowardice wasn't the worst kind there was. Luke's words spun in her head like clay on a potter's wheel. Answers from her heart shaped the clay.

*Stop running and face your fears.*

She'd always said she didn't want to hurt Luke and Gor-die, but that wasn't true. What she really wanted was to protect herself from being hurt.

*When the time comes, I hope you'll deal yourself a good hand.*

She'd chosen not to play at all. Opting for the easiest way out, she'd convinced herself love and hope just weren't enough. Commitment took courage.

*Life doesn't come with any guarantees . . . all it gives us is opportunities.*

She had to believe she would use those opportunities in the right way.

The wheel stopped spinning. She was left with one sim-ple, beautiful fact.

What she really needed, now, was faith. In herself, in Luke, in their love. Faith that she and Luke would do their best to make their marriage work . . . faith that it would.

It was all anyone ever had.

"Faith." Rachel savored the word even as she thought about it.

It was the last vital ingredient her recipe for happiness had lacked. Until now.

"Hannah." Both women turned startled faces to her as she whirled into the kitchen, her hair wild, her eyes overly large in her flushed face.

"Is something wrong?" Hannah wasn't really alarmed. Rachel's face was glowing as if lit from within. Hannah had no problem identifying love when she saw it.

"Are you all right?" Theresa's brow was knitted in worry.

"Nothing's wrong." Rachel thrust their concern aside, her expression allaying any doubts. "Nothing bad's happened. I must talk to Luke right away. Where's the number he left with you?"

"By the telephone in his study, but he might not . . ." Hannah's voice trailed away as Rachel flew into the study and shut the door.

Gordie looked at the study door and then at Hannah. For the first time since the day she'd picked him up, he had been bypassed without a hug or a kiss. "Nana, Mama gone?" he asked, looking at the study door.

Hannah stared at him, speechless. Talk about winning the Triple Crown. Her gaze collided with Theresa's. Her own shock was reflected there. Three words and strung together so well. And he'd called her Nana! She couldn't have thought up a sweeter title, herself. That wasn't all. From the look on Rachel's face all would soon be well between her and Luke.

Picking Gordie up, she hugged him to her breast. Over his head she exchanged a beaming, teary smile with Theresa.

"No," she informed the youngest Summer, "I don't think your new mama is going anywhere."

Raising her eyes upwards, she said reproachfully, "But that was a mighty close call. You might remember I'm getting too old for cliff-hangers."

Rachel ran her fingers through her hair as she heard the telephone ring at the other end, looking surprised at the pine needle between her fingers.

Five. Six times. She shifted uneasily. He wasn't there.

Luke picked it up on the ninth ring.

"Yes?"

He didn't sound too encouraging. Rachel drew a deep breath and then plunged into her speech.

"Luke, it's me . . . Rachel. Please don't say a word till I finish talking. Luke, it's hit me all of a sudden. I can't leave you or Gordie. I love you. Deep down inside, I know I've always felt that some day, somewhere, I would meet a man who would change my life with his love. There was always hope and then you offered me your love. I've loved you right from the moment I opened my eyes in the guest room and you were there. All I needed was faith. Faith in myself. Faith that our marriage will work because we both intend to do our best to ensure it does. I have that now." The utter silence from the other end alarmed her. "Luke?" Maybe she had the wrong number. Maybe Luke didn't want her, after all. "Luke, are you there?"

"I'm here." He was breathing as if he'd just finished a marathon. "Are you sure, Rae?"

"I'm sure, Luke . . . that is if you still want me?"

"Want you?" He groaned. "I've gone out of my mind wanting you and waiting for you to make just this move."

"You knew I would?"

"I hoped, darling."

The edges of uncertainty blurred and vanished at the love in Luke's voice.

"Oh, Luke, I love you. I've wasted so much time. I'm sorry." Tears streamed down her face and ran into her voice.

"Are you crying again?"

"Yes." Rachel nodded before she realized Luke couldn't see her, "But it's only because I'm so ha . . . happy. I don't know why you love me . . ."

She was interrupted sternly. "No more of that, Rae. I'm a very lucky man."

"If you say so. I want to hear more about that, later."

A spurt of mischief came through clearly in the teasing note in her voice, gladdening Luke's heart. He wanted to fill her life with so much sunshine that the shadows never dared return.

"What I wouldn't give to have you in my arms this very minute, Rae." The huskiness in Luke's voice sent a tremor of delight through her.

"Me, too," Rachel said softly.

"I'm not sorry you called, but you sure pick a unique time to propose to a guy. I can't touch you or see your face."

"When are you coming back?" Rachel demanded. "This isn't a real proposal. I want it done the right way. Moonlight, roses and you beside me."

"You'll have it all." The silken, love wrapped threat made her tremble in delicious anticipation. "I'll be back by tonight."

"I'll have to call Dr. Smith and let him know I won't be on that plane." All at once she was shy. Words might help. "Wish I'd known earlier...I'd have saved myself all the trouble of having those shots. Hannah's going to be so happy."

"*Everyone's* going to be so happy," Luke said. "I'm going to contact Reverend Hanson and ask him to marry us at the ranch tomorrow."

"Tomorrow?" Rachel squeaked, "isn't that too soon?"

"No," Luke said firmly. "I've been patient long enough. I'm starting the New Year with my wife. That's unless you don't want to...?"

But Rachel had lost time to make up for, as well. "I want to," she interrupted firmly, "very much."

"I asked Dr. Kenton to do a blood test on me a couple of weeks ago," Luke said, "and then just in case you changed your mind, I got a special license and talked to Reverend Hanson."

"Well!" And she'd had to spend sleepless nights and countless hours worrying to come up with the answer. "You might have told me if you were so sure of the outcome."

"That was the one thing I couldn't do for you, sweetheart." Luke's tone was deadly serious. "Don't you see? For our marriage to succeed you had to make your own decision. Not that the waiting was easy. Besides, there was a time when I thought I'd lost you just by being so damned noble. Hannah didn't help either, serving up boiled carrots every night and muttering about laggards in love."

Rachel laughed. Her wonderful, gallant, patient knight in shining armor. "There's so much to do. I have to help Hannah and Theresa get things ready for tomorrow. It's going to be too much for them to do overnight."

"You're not going to do a thing," Luke interrupted firmly. "The wedding lunch will be catered by a firm in Santa Barbara, which has an excellent reputation. I'll call them right away. We'll just have Hannah, Betty and Bud, the Rodriguez family and Jason. Is that okay with you?" At her murmur of assent, he said, "Later, when Dad gets back from his cruise, we'll have a big reception."

"Let's have Mojo, too." Fairy godmothers came in various forms these days. Her thoughts went off at a tangent. "I don't have a dress to wear. Maybe Jason can drive me down to Santa Barbara.

"Relax," Luke ordered. "Hannah and Theresa mentioned that all three of you went through the family wedding dresses one day and you seemed to love my mother's. Well, they had it cleaned and told me it would fit you perfectly with half an hour's work on it."

"Honestly!" Her protest sounded weak. She didn't really mind the arrangements. She was lucky to have found so many people who cared about her.

"We'll get you a trousseau after the honeymoon."

"We're not really going away on a honeymoon, are we?" She couldn't think of a better place to spend the first weeks of her married life than at the Diamond Bar.

"Yes, we are," Luke said firmly. "The destination's secret and I don't want to hear a word about Gordie. Betty and Bud will stay on at the ranch till we return and he'll be just fine. We need this time alone with each other."

"Yes, Luke," Rachel said meekly.

"Are you laughing at me?" he demanded suspiciously.

"Who, me?" Rachel asked with mock innocence. "I wouldn't dream of it."

Time enough to tell him her plans for a large family would keep them very busy in the years to come. Gordie was going to have a passel of brothers and sisters.

"You have a nice long nap and wait for me," Luke ordered huskily, his happiness coming over the wires as clearly as if he were in front of her.

"Wait up for you? Why?" Rachel asked mischievously.

And her unofficial fiancé proceeded to tell her exactly why.

He found her in the sun room. Being able to charter a small plane had saved quite a bit of time. The single lamp she'd turned on bathed the room in a rosy glow. The movement of the rocker told him she was in it. Wisps of a song floated to him over the back. He stood there letting her music flood his being, praying he would always have her to come home to.

Angela brushed past him, mumbled something to Rae, took Gordie out of her arms and rushed out of the room, closing the door, a huge grin splitting her face. No one else was around. Evidently everyone had their instructions.

Rachel stood up, turning to see where Gordie was being taken in such a hurry. She saw him and froze.

Luke waited. Had she changed her mind?

"Luke?" Her smile still held a tinge of uncertainty.

"Rae." His voice came out hoarse, unlike himself, betraying his fear.

She ran to him, flung herself into his waiting arms, clinging to him as if she would never let him go. "I love you, Luke."

The assurance of her love was there in her touch. In her face. It shone through her eyes and he knew she was giving herself to him, body, mind and soul.

"I love you, sweetheart."

Their lips met in sweet token of the promise of eternity. And Luke knew they would spend the rest of their lives celebrating their love.

\*    \*    \*    \*    \*

# Silhouette Romance

## COMING NEXT MONTH

**#730 BORROWED BABY—Marie Ferrarella**
*A Diamond Jubilee Book!*
Stuck with a six-month-old bundle of joy, reserved policeman Griff Foster became a petrified parent. Then bubbly Liz MacDougall taught him a thing or two about diapers, teething, lullabies and love.

**#731 FULL BLOOM—Karen Leabo**
When free-spirited Hilary McShane returned early from her vacation, she hadn't expected to find methodical Matthew Burke as a substitute house-sitter. Their life-styles and attitudes clashed, but their love kept growing....

**#732 THAT MAN NEXT DOOR—Judith Bowen**
New dairy owner Caitlin Forrest was entranced by friendly neighbor Ben Wade. When she discovered that he wanted her farm, however, she wondered exactly how much business he was mixing with pleasure.

**#733 HOME FIRES BURNING BRIGHT—Laurie Paige**
**Book II of HOMEWARD BOUND DUO**
Carson McCumber felt he had nothing to offer a woman—especially privileged Tess Garrick. Out to prove the rugged rancher wrong, Tess was determined to keep all the home fires burning....

**#734 BETTER TO HAVE LOVED—Linda Varner**
Convinced she'd lose, loner Allison Kendall had vowed never to play the game of love. But martial-arts enthusiast Meade Duran was an expert at tearing down all kinds of defenses.

**#735 VENUS de MOLLY—Peggy Webb**
Cool, controlled banker Samuel Adams became hot under the collar when he thought about his mother marrying Molly Rakestraw's father. But that was before he met the irrepressible Molly!

## AVAILABLE THIS MONTH:

**#724 CIMARRON KNIGHT**
Pepper Adams

**#725 FEARLESS FATHER**
Terry Essig

**#726 FAITH, HOPE and LOVE**
Geeta Kingsley

**#727 A SEASON FOR HOMECOMING**
Laurie Paige

**#728 FAMILY MAN**
Arlene James

**#THE SEDUCTION OF ANNA**
Brittany Young

*Silhouette Romance*®

## *A duo by Laurie Paige*

There's no place like home—and Laurie Paige's delightful duo captures that heartwarming feeling in two special stories set in Arizona ranchland. Share the poignant homecomings of two lovely heroines—half sisters Lainie and Tess—as they travel on the road to romance with their rugged, handsome heroes.

A SEASON FOR HOMECOMING—Lainie and Dev's story...available now.

HOME FIRES BURNING BRIGHT—Tess and Carson's story...coming in July.

Come home to A SEASON FOR HOMECOMING (#727) and HOME FIRES BURNING BRIGHT (#733)...only from Silhouette Romance!

---

A SEASON FOR HOMECOMING (#727) is available now at your favorite retail outlet or order your copy by sending your name, address, and zip or postal code along with a check or money order for $2.25, plus 75¢ postage and handling, payable to Silhouette Reader Service to:

In the U.S.
901 Fuhrmann Blvd.
P.O. Box 1396
Buffalo, NY 14269-1396

In Canada
P.O. Box 609
Fort Erie, Ontario
L2A 5X3

Please specify book title with your order.

HB-1A

# Take 4 bestselling love stories FREE

## Plus get a FREE surprise gift!

## Special Limited-time Offer

Mail to    **Silhouette Reader Service®**

In the U.S.                In Canada
901 Fuhrmann Blvd.         P.O. Box 609
P.O. Box 1867             Fort Erie, Ontario
Buffalo, N.Y. 14269-1867   L2A 5X3

**YES!** Please send me 4 free Silhouette Romance® novels and my free surprise gift. Then send me 6 brand-new novels every month, which I will receive months before they appear in bookstores. Bill me at the already low price of $2.25* each. There are no shipping, handling or other hidden costs. I understand that accepting these books and gifts places me under no obligation ever to buy any books. I can always return a shipment and cancel at any time. Even if I never buy another book from Silhouette, the 4 free books and the surprise gift are mine to keep forever.

* Offer slightly different in Canada—$2.25 per book plus 69¢ per shipment for delivery.

Sales tax applicable in N.Y. and Iowa.                315 BPA 8176  (CAN)
215 BPA HAYY (US)

Name                    (PLEASE PRINT)

Address                                  Apt. No.

City              State/Prov.         Zip/Postal Code

This offer is limited to one order per household and not valid to present Silhouette Romance® subscribers. Terms and prices are subject to change.

© 1990 Harlequin Enterprises Limited

*Silhouette Romance*®

CIMARRON STORIES

# A TRILOGY BY PEPPER ADAMS

Pepper Adams is back and spicier than ever with three tender, heartwarming tales, set on the plains of Oklahoma.

**CIMARRON KNIGHT** ... available in June
Rugged rancher and dyed-in-the-wool bachelor Brody Sawyer meets his match in determined Noelle Chandler and her adorable twin boys!

**CIMARRON GLORY** ... available in August
With a stubborn streak as strong as her foster brother Brody's, Glory Roberts has her heart set on lassoing handsome loner Ross Forbes ... and uncovering his mysterious past....

**CIMARRON REBEL** ... available in October
Brody's brother Riley is a handsome rebel with a cause! And he doesn't mind getting roped into marrying Darcy Durant—in name only—to gain custody of two heartbroken kids.

Don't miss CIMARRON KNIGHT, CIMARRON GLORY and
CIMARRON REBEL—three special stories that'll win your
heart ... available only from Silhouette Romance!

Look for these titles at your favorite retail outlet, or order your copy by sending your name, address, zip or postal code along with a check or money order for $2.25, plus 75¢ postage and handling, payable to Silhouette Reader Service to:

In the U.S.
901 Fuhrmann Blvd.
Box 1396
Buffalo, NY 14269-1396
Please specify book title(s) with your order.

In Canada
P.O. Box 609
Fort Erie, Ontario
L2A 5X3

CIM-1A

# 🖤 *Diamond Jubilee Collection*

## It's our 10th Anniversary... and *you* get a present!

This collection of early Silhouette Romances features novels written by three of your favorite authors:

**ANN MAJOR**—*Wild Lady*
**ANNETTE BROADRICK**—*Circumstantial Evidence*
**DIXIE BROWNING**—*Island on the Hill*

* **These Silhouette Romance titles were first published in the early 1980s and have not been available since!**

* **Beautiful Collector's Edition bound in antique green simulated leather to last a lifetime!**

* **Embossed in gold on the cover and spine!**

✂ PROOF OF PURCHASE

This special collection will not be sold in retail stores and is only available through this exclusive offer:

Send your name, address and zip or postal code, along with six proof-of-purchase coupons from any Silhouette Romance published in June, July and/or August, plus $2.50 for postage and handling (check or money order—please do not send cash) payable to Silhouette Reader Service to:

| In the U.S. | In Canada |
|---|---|
| Free Book Offer | Free Book Offer |
| Silhouette Books | Silhouette Books |
| 901 Fuhrmann Blvd. | P.O. Box 609 |
| Box 9055 | Fort Erie, Ontario |
| Buffalo, NY  14269-9055 | L2A 5X3 |

(Please allow 4-6 weeks for delivery. Hurry! Quantities are limited. Offer expires September 30, 1990.)

DJC-1A